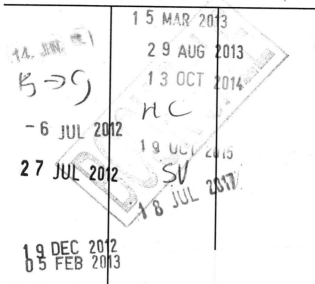

The Search for the Lone Star

It had long been rumored that the fabulous diamond known as the Lone Star had been buried somewhere near the town of Diamond Springs. Many men had died trying to claim it, but when Diamond Springs became a ghost town, the men who went there had many different aims. Tex Callahan had been paid to complete a mission, Rafferty Horn wanted to put right a past mistake, George Milligan thought he knew what had happened to the diamond, and Elias Sutherland wanted revenge.

All were united by their hatred of Creswell Washington, a man who had cast a dark shadow over all their lives during his search for the diamond. Only after violent retribution will the truth be finally revealed about the Lone Star.

By the same author

The Outlawed Deputy
The Last Rider from Hell
Death or Bounty
Bad Day in Dirtwood
Devine's Law
Yates's Dilemma
The Ten Per Cent Gang
Mendosa's Gun-runners
Wanted: McBain
Six-shooter Bride
Dead by Sundown
Calhoun's Bounty
Calloway's Crossing
Bad Moon over Devil's Ridge
Massacre at Bluff Point
The Gallows Gang
Riders of the Barren Plains
Sharpshooter McClure
Railroad to Redemption
Bleached Bones in the Dust
The Secret of Devil's Canyon
The Prairie Man
Sheriff Without a Star

The Search for the Lone Star

I.J. Parnham

A Black Horse Western

ROBERT HALE · LONDON

ISBN 978-0-7090-9303-9

Robert Hale Limited
Clerkenwell House
Clerkenwell Green
London EC1R 0HT

www.halebooks.com

Typeset by
Derek Doyle & Associates, Shaw Heath
Printed and bound in Great Britain by
CPI Antony Rowe, Chippenham and Eastbourne

CHAPTER 1

'Next stop, Diamond Springs!'

The declaration made the passenger facing Tex Callahan peer out of the window. The third man in the stage was asleep, as he had been since they'd left Monotony.

'Don't worry, Elias,' Tex said. 'It'll be a short stop. You'll still get to Bear Creek before noon.'

'But the stage doesn't stop at Diamond Springs,' Elias Sutherland said.

Tex smiled. 'That changes today.'

He cast Elias a narrow-eyed glare, defying him to continue offering complaints, although his reaction had been the same as the driver's. That debate had ended when Tex had handed over ten dollars.

Tex hadn't minded. For the amount he was being paid, he'd have gladly given him a hundred dollars.

While Elias shook his head in bemusement, he looked out of the window, but the swirling dust that the stage had been kicking up for the last few miles still marred his view.

A saddle-bag was at his feet and he swung it over a shoulder. He always travelled with the minimum of luggage, but even so, he'd brought the bag into the stage when he'd paid the driver.

When they stopped he would need to move quickly, and standing around waiting for his luggage to be thrown down could be the last mistake he'd make.

The changing tempo of the rattling wheels let him judge that they would be stopping within a minute. So he tipped his hat to Elias and then concentrated on getting out with the minimum of fuss.

The moment the stage lurched to a halt, he was on his feet. With a lithe movement he opened the door and jumped down. The dust had yet to settle and that was fine with Tex.

'I said I'd drop you off on the edge of town,' the driver shouted as he leaned to the side to look down at him. 'But you can still change your mind.'

'Nope,' Tex said as he moved to the back of the stage.

'Then that's your choice, but I'll be back this way in a few days. I can stop off and—'

'Get moving!' Tex muttered. His gaze had centred on a large building that was emerging from behind the dust and the sight added urgency to his demand.

The driver muttered under his breath. Then, with

a crack of his whip, he trundled the stage off towards Bear Creek, making the dust swirl and blocking off Tex's view of the building.

Tex moved sideways, following the path of the stage to keep himself hidden from anyone who might be watching for a few more seconds. Then he halted and waited.

Repeatedly, the dust coalesced and thinned, giving him brief flashes of the large building as the stage rattled away until in a moment the dust cleared, to leave him with uninterrupted vision.

The building was an abandoned shell. Then again, he had alighted on the edge of town. He turned to face down the main drag.

He saw more of the same.

Most of the buildings were hollowed-out skeletons. Some buildings had been burnt down, others had fallen down, and there was no sign of any living person amidst the dust and the sun-baked dirt.

To his side the rotting town sign confirmed that the driver had, in fact, dropped him off in Diamond Springs. The sign stood at an angle looking as if a strong wind would topple it.

The fading legend claimed that at one time seventy-five people had lived here, but the number had been crossed out and a large zero had been painted in red. Even the paint was flaking.

Tex shrugged and, with a roll of the shoulders, he headed on into town.

7

Rafferty Horn moved to push open the door, but then he changed his mind and gestured for his massive associate to carry out the task in his usual manner. Accordingly, Bud took a giant step forward and kicked the door with the sole of his boot.

The door split in two.

Rafferty put on a welcoming smile. Then he slipped past Bud and stepped neatly between the two halves as they fell to the floor.

Inside, Oliver Lee was standing in the centre of his main room, fingering a short, thick log with menace, but his downcast gaze showed that he knew the puny weapon wouldn't save him.

'Fifty dollars,' Rafferty said using his most pleasant tone. 'Now.'

'You know I haven't got it,' Oliver babbled, sweat breaking out on his forehead. 'I told you yesterday. I surely did. There's nothing else I can do.'

'Except there's a rumour going round that you got lucky in a poker game.'

Oliver's eyes opened wide and his mouth fell open, showing surprise in a way that Rafferty reckoned he couldn't feign. As Oliver struggled to find an answer, Bud lumbered along to stand at Rafferty's shoulder. The closeness of the huge man made Oliver shake so much the log shed bark.

'I don't play poker,' Oliver said at last. He gestured

behind him at the ajar door to another room. His wife was peering through the gap. Two children were clutching her skirts and demanding to know what was happening. 'I can't when I have a family to support.'

Oliver lowered the log. Then he spread his arms and put on a pleading expression, but his eyes remained sad showing that he knew he had no hope of clemency.

Rafferty smiled and then frowned, trying to appear as if he were pondering on Oliver's fate, while Bud remained impassive, but then again, he rarely acted in an animated manner.

The tense moment lasted for only thirty seconds, but it was long enough for the beads of sweat on Oliver's brow to coalesce into a droplet that slid down to his cheek and then jaw where it dangled before falling.

'Bud,' Rafferty said, speaking softly, 'rearrange the furniture.'

As Bud rolled his substantial shoulders and stepped forward, Oliver raised the log to shoulder height and swung the weapon in an arc towards Bud's head.

With a casual gesture Bud raised a hand and caught the log, halting it so suddenly the rest of the bark rained down on him. Then he yanked the crude weapon from Oliver's grasp and hefted it in his own hand ready to use it as a cudgel.

'Obliged,' he intoned. His voice was deep, but after working with Bud for two years, Rafferty could tell that he'd found the change of situation amusing.

Oliver advanced on him with his fists rising, but Bud had already dismissed him from his thoughts. With a bored gesture, he slapped a meaty palm against Oliver's face, flattening his nose while wrapping the fingers so far around his cheeks that they stretched beyond the ears.

Bud shoved, making Oliver go wheeling away for two paces before he slipped and went sliding all his length to come to a halt against the wall.

Bud got to work.

Swinging the log back and forth as if it were nothing more than a twig, he proceeded to demolish everything Oliver had worked to achieve.

The stew in the pot that stood before the fire splashed against the wall, while the pot broke through the window shutters. Plates on the table went flying and then the table itself went tumbling.

Oliver had enough sense not to get in Bud's way; instead he clambered to his feet to stand before Rafferty. He wiped blood away from his nose, then raised his hands in a pleading gesture.

'Give it to me,' Rafferty said.

'I haven't got no money,' Oliver murmured. He cast a forlorn look at the destruction Bud was wreaking. 'You're right. I did play poker, but I was desperate and I only won enough to feed my family for another week. The money's gone now.'

This admission had the ring of truth, so Rafferty glanced at Bud, seeing that he had his back to him as he converted the table to firewood. With an eye on Bud, he reached into an inside pocket, withdrew an envelope, and thrust it into Oliver's hands.

'I said,' Rafferty demanded, speaking loudly, 'give it to me, now!'

Oliver stared at the envelope with his eyes narrowed and confused. Then, with a shrug, he opened it to see the wad of bills inside.

He jerked his head up to look at Rafferty. A silent question was on his lips, but when Rafferty folded his arms, he stopped questioning his luck.

'Stop!' he bleated. 'I'll give you the money.'

Bud brought the log down again, splitting the table, then turned as Oliver held out the envelope.

Rafferty reached over to the envelope and withdrew the money. He carefully counted through it with his eyebrows raised as if he hadn't expected this capitulation.

'It'd seem that you've now repaid your debt,' he said. 'Don't hold out on me again.'

'I . . . I . . . won't,' Oliver murmured, searching Rafferty's eyes for an explanation, 'but I sure won't ever get into debt to Creswell Washington again.'

'They all say that.'

Rafferty removed Creswell's debt book from his pocket and, with a grand gesture that made Oliver smile, he made an obvious tick. He turned the book around and indicated the spot where Oliver should sign, his attitude now businesslike. Then he backed away while smiling and waded through the debris that Bud had created.

As he left, he heard consternation growing back in the house as Oliver's wife emerged from hiding to ask the inevitable questions, so he moved away briskly in case Bud overheard what they said.

Not that Bud would mention the matter if it concerned him. Bud wasn't the type for conversation, but ten minutes later when Rafferty headed into the Dark Night Saloon on the main drag through Bear Creek, Creswell Washington was certainly in the mood to talk.

Creswell ushered him away from the half-filled saloon room to his upstairs office. As usual, he bade Bud wait outside in the corridor to ensure they weren't disturbed.

Creswell moved over to stand at his office window where he looked down on what he viewed as being his domain. Even in the early afternoon the road was bustling with activity.

On the window an arc proclaimed Creswell's name and he stood beneath it, tapping fist against palm behind his back. He stood for so long without speaking that he would have made Rafferty uncomfortable, if it weren't for the fact that Rafferty also made people wait when he was in the superior position.

'Everyone pay?' Creswell asked, still looking down at the road.

'Everyone,' Rafferty said, 'even Oliver Lee, although Bud had to demolish half his house first.'

Rafferty threw Creswell's debt book on to his desk, followed by an envelope containing a wad of bills. The noise made Creswell glance over his shoulder. He gave the book a cursory look but ignored the money.

'That's welcome. It'll help to replenish my dwindling fortune.'

'The businesses not doing so well, then?'

'They are.' Creswell turned. 'But money's gone missing from my safe, again.'

'How much?' Rafferty said levelly.

Creswell looked down at the wad of bills, his brow furrowed with suppressed anger.

'The amount's irrelevant. The fact that someone I trust stole from me isn't. When I find the culprit he'll lose my trust, and after Mitch Sawyer has finished with him, he'll have lost his ability to enjoy life.'

'I understand. Do you want me to find out who did it?'

'I don't need your help,' Creswell said, his tone lowering with menace. 'I've already put measures in place to find out who's gone and got himself a death wish. After the last time it happened, I made small tears in some of my bills. When I see those tears again, I'll question the man who owns them.'

13

Creswell offered a thin smile, then left the window and slipped down behind his desk. He stretched a hand for the envelope while keeping his gaze on Rafferty, his blank expression inviting him to speak, but Rafferty couldn't think of anything he could say.

Creswell withdrew the first bill and considered it, then he looked at the second.

Rafferty cast his mind back, but he couldn't remember seeing any torn bills when he'd given the money to Creswell's debtors, so this could be a bluff. If it wasn't, he was more familiar than most with how Creswell would react.

On the other hand, he'd worked for Creswell for two years. He might be able to talk himself out of this situation, but only if he spoke up now.

'Wait,' he said.

Creswell looked up, the third bill half-withdrawn from the envelope.

'For what?'

Rafferty tried to reply, but his mouth had gone dry. As he struggled to find the right thing to say, rapid footfalls sounded in the corridor outside.

'Sounds like trouble,' he said with relief at getting an unexpected distraction.

Creswell narrowed his eyes, but when the door burst open he looked past Rafferty. One of his workers, Wiley Gaunt, had arrived, although as Bud had grabbed him around the waist he stayed in the doorway.

'I'm busy,' Creswell said.

'But there's a problem,' Wiley said. His voice was gruff, showing that being the bearer of bad news had scared him, as it should.

'I'd gathered.' Creswell gave Rafferty a long look that promised he wouldn't be distracted into forgetting this matter. 'I hope for your sake it's serious.'

'It is. The stage is late and Sheriff Bryce went scouting around to see if there'd been any trouble. He's just got back and it's terrible news. Elias's not on it.'

Creswell slammed his fist on the desk, flipping the envelope over and sending the bills fluttering away.

'I wanted to end this matter today.'

'You didn't get what I meant,' Wiley said, wringing his hands. 'It's not just that he's not on the stage. Nobody else is on it either. The carriage is standing there outside town and there's not nobody on it at all!'

15

CHAPTER 2

Wiley Gaunt's announcement that the stage had been deserted turned out to be not entirely accurate.

When Rafferty Horn and Creswell Washington located Sheriff Bryce outside the law office, he confirmed that the carriage had been abandoned outside town. Strangely, it was also several miles away from its usual route.

The driver had gone, as had Elias, but one passenger had still been on board. He had been asleep and he had claimed to be surprised when he'd found himself the subject of the lawman's interest.

With the sheriff not believing he could have slept through an event that had led to the other passenger disappearing, Bryce had arrested him on suspicion of being involved in the incident.

'How long are you keeping your prisoner?'

Creswell asked.

'Until he becomes co-operative,' Bryce said, 'and convinces me he's not involved in whatever happened out there.'

'If you want answers, I'll get them.'

Bryce raised a hand in a warding off gesture while snorting a harsh laugh.

'I'm sure you could, but I like my prisoners still to be alive when they leave my care.' Bryce considered him. 'So why was Elias coming here?'

Creswell provided an ingratiating smile. 'I'm always keen to help the law. He's a respected business associate of mine.'

Bryce snorted. 'Never try bluffing at poker, Creswell. Even Oliver Lee could tell you're lying.'

Before Creswell could retort, the sheriff headed into the law office, leaving Creswell glaring at the closed door with his fists opening and closing. When he regained his composure, he drew Rafferty aside to walk with him back to the Dark Night saloon.

'That lawman is getting too many ideas these days,' he said.

'I reckon he thinks he runs the law.'

Rafferty had meant his comment to be sarcastic, but Creswell nodded.

'I know, and the sooner this town gets a lawman who knows his place the better.' Creswell pointed towards the place where the stage had been left. 'For now, use your old investigating skills and get me some answers about what's happened to Elias Sutherland.'

Rafferty winced when he heard Elias's full name for the first time.

'That would be Loudon Sutherland's brother from Diamond Springs?'

'It would.' Creswell stopped outside his saloon to consider him, his sly smile showing that Rafferty's discomfiture amused him. 'So as you can imagine, I'm keen to know what's happened to him.'

'I understand. Do you want me to bring him back dead or alive?'

'Alive. I want answers.' Creswell withdrew the bills he'd been examining earlier from his pocket. He peeled off several and glanced at them. 'And while you're finding him, Mitch can devote his time to working out who's discovered the combination to my safe.'

Rafferty met Creswell's eye. 'I wish him luck.'

Creswell extracted a bill with an obvious tear at the side and held the bill aloft, ensuring that Rafferty saw the rip. Then he stuffed it along with several others into Rafferty's pocket.

'For expenses,' he said. 'Don't disappoint me.'

Without further comment Creswell headed inside, but Rafferty didn't need to be told anything more.

Creswell now had him. In truth, for the last two years he'd had him in the palm of his hand, but now that his attempt to curtail Creswell's worst excesses had been uncovered, the hand was ready to tighten into an iron grip around him.

So he set about satisfying his master's orders by collecting Bud from where he'd been left outside Creswell's office. They joined Deputy Gordon Haywood's group, which was heading out of town to collect the stage. These four men were eager to see at first hand the source of a mystery that everyone in town would be talking about come sundown.

Rafferty didn't join in the chatter. Bud was silent as usual.

Five miles out of town they reached the stage. It proved to be as incongruous a sight as they'd been led to believe. The carriage stood alone on the plains, the horses were gone, the only movement being the open doors swinging back and forth in the breeze.

Haywood told everyone to stay back while he dismounted and viewed the scene from all angles. When he returned he reported that there were no obvious signs of an attack having been carried out.

There were a few hoofprints that had probably been made by the sheriff when he'd found the stage. Other than that, the area didn't appear to have been even visited.

'It's as if the stage just appeared here,' Haywood said as he invited the other three men to hitch up their horses to take the stage back to town.

'Not even prints from the horses when they were

run off or stolen?' Rafferty asked.

'No, but we should at least be able to see them.' Haywood frowned. 'Someone must have brushed them away. And if they brushed those prints away, they could have removed more.'

'I reckon this mystery will get less mysterious the more we look.' Rafferty pointed to the stage roof. 'The luggage has gone too, so perhaps this was nothing more than a simple raid.'

Haywood gestured for Wiley Gaunt to climb up and check. Wiley confirmed that no possessions had been left, so Haywood rooted around inside the coach. He emerged shaking his head, then came over to join Rafferty, where he considered Bud and then him.

'What was Elias Sutherland's business?' he asked, keeping his voice low so that the others couldn't hear, so giving Rafferty the chance to confide in him.

'I don't know, honestly.' Rafferty watched Haywood shake his head. 'You can trust me on that, Gordon.'

Haywood snorted. 'I might once have believed you, but not now. And that's Deputy Haywood to you.'

'Understood, Deputy Haywood.'

Rafferty turned away, aiming to look around the stage and see if he could find anything interesting that Haywood had missed, but Haywood coughed making him turn back.

'What's happened to you, Rafferty?' he asked, his tone weary. 'You were once a decent man. You even used to do my job before you went to work for Creswell.'

'Don't believe everything you've heard about what happened when I was Sheriff Bryce's deputy.'

'I don't. I make up my own mind and I've seen Creswell chip away at the man you once were. And now you're doing his dirty work for him again.'

'I work for him, but that doesn't mean I'm dirty too.'

'It does. Increasingly, every theft and every shooting in Bear Creek leads back to Creswell. So Sheriff Bryce and I have vowed that what happened to Diamond Springs won't happen here. We can't prove nothing right now, but one day soon Creswell will make a mistake and we'll be waiting for him. And do you know what'll happen then?'

'What?'

Haywood walked up to Rafferty to look him in the eye. Rafferty stood his ground.

'He'll hire the best lawyers he can buy. Then he'll distance himself from the trouble and blame it on someone else, someone expendable.' He looked Rafferty up and down with unconcealed contempt. 'Someone like you.'

Rafferty couldn't think of a reply because Haywood was right; that was how Creswell operated. So when Haywood turned away to organize taking the stage to town, Rafferty stood back.

As nobody spoke to him again, Rafferty didn't feel inclined to trail on behind the entourage. When the stage moved off, he stood in a position where he could enjoy respite from the sun in Bud's vast shadow.

'Where now, Bud?' he asked when the stage had receded into the distance.

The question had been rhetorical as his hulking partner rarely spoke, and when he did he never provided helpful advice. Decisions were Rafferty's responsibility while Bud got involved only when violence was required.

'Find Elias,' Bud intoned, using his slow drawl that enunciated every consonant as if they all required an enormous force of will to produce.

He had only stated the obvious, but it was a welcome comment. Rafferty considered the distant stage. It was going west, the direction it had been pointed and a direction along which it shouldn't have come. He looked east.

'The only nearby town that way is Diamond Springs.' He glanced at Bud, but the big man gave no sign that the possibilities aroused his curiosity in the way they had Rafferty's. 'The stage came from over there. So something interesting has to be that way. Let's find out what it is.'

Rafferty and Bud mounted up. When they rode out they headed east towards the ghost town that held only bad memories of the time when Rafferty had become the man he was now, a man who hated himself.

CHAPTER 3

Diamond Springs was a ghost town and it had been for some time.

Tex Callahan had reached this conclusion after exploring the buildings and surrounding area. This discovery hadn't worried him, merely made him curious as to why he'd been paid to come here in the first place.

Accordingly, he searched for shade from the high sun and found it in one of the few complete buildings, which had once been a saloon. A fallen sign outside proclaimed that it had been the Lone Star saloon. Its legend had faded and bullet holes marked the outline of the background star.

He failed to find an intact chair, so he settled down in the doorway with his shoulders resting on one jamb and a raised foot set on the other.

From here he would notice any movement outside while he considered the letter that had invited him.

He flicked it open and read the few terse sentences.

Even though he now knew how the journey had panned out, it didn't help him to put a different slant on the instructions that had provided only the payment offer and details about which stage to take. As patience was one of the requirements of his job, he assumed that soon someone would come and explain why he'd been called to this abandoned town.

With no sign of that person arriving yet, he got to his feet and wandered around the derelict saloon, looking for something to occupy his mind. His gaze alighted on the bar.

A bottle of whiskey stood there. Beside it was a dusty glass and both items rested on a leather-bound book, which was also dusty.

Tex ignored the whiskey and took the book back to the doorway where he adopted the same posture as before. He opened it and discovered that it was a diary.

This is a true account, Tex read, *of the events leading up to the terrible day that destroyed a forgotten town.*

Tex read on. He took his time while he cast frequent glances up and down the deserted road.

The diary contained entries that had been written late at night by a man called George Milligan. After an hour Tex had read half the diary and although he hadn't found out why he'd been enticed here, the developing situation gripped his interest.

George had run the saloon in which he now sat. Every night he had detailed the evening's events, painting an entertaining picture of his colourful customers' antics.

Tex noticed recurring themes, such as the saloon-room rumour that an outlaw gang had holed up near by. As it turned out, this rumour hadn't amounted to anything, as most of the other rumours and tales that the customers told over a whiskey every evening.

One rumour didn't die out.

Tex had first noted it a quarter of the way through the diary, and every few days more details were added. It concerned the town's oldest and most popular rumour: that the reason the town had been called Diamond Springs was because a fabulous diamond known as the Lone Star had been buried near by.

This gem had come from a stash of old pirate treasure. Apparently, the diamond was so large and bright that it glowed like a star and legend said that it had fallen from the sky to become a glittering piece of heaven on earth.

Ultimately, the diamond had ended up in the Texas Republic, where a proud Texan had given the gem its current name. The thought made Tex's heart quicken and he couldn't help but smile as he wondered what the Lone Star looked like.

Later, the rumour went on, during the Mexican War invading soldiers had seized it. Then bandits had killed the soldiers.

The bandits had headed north, eventually fetching up in what was now Kansas. With capture imminent, they had buried the diamond near to the springs. Then everyone who had known its exact location had died in a ferocious gunfight.

Tex had heard plenty of tales like this one, and so had the customers, so, like him they had greeted the rumour with scorn.

He had started reading the most promising entry so far, in which a customer had claimed he now knew the location of the Lone Star and would divulge it in return for free whiskey, when movement caught his attention.

Tex looked up to see that three riders were coming towards him from the direction in which the stage had gone. They were still a quarter-mile away, so Tex moved leisurely.

He took the diary inside and placed it back on the bar beside the unopened whiskey bottle and the glass. Then, as an afterthought, he marked the progress of his reading by folding down the corner of a page. Then he returned to take up a position leaning against the side of the doorway and looking out of town.

The riders were no longer visible.

Tex winced, then risked moving out through the saloon doorway, but he still couldn't see them. He had been inside for only a minute, so they must have moved quickly, anticipating his actions in a way that he could only view as being suspicious.

Tex backed away to the saloon wall. Then he skirted around it and entered the derelict building that stood alongside.

The walls had fallen in, masking the function the place had once had and the wood and other debris had rotten down so much they had formed a powdery deposit. But this left plenty of open spaces so Tex could see in all directions while the remnants of the walls still provided some cover.

Bent double, he scurried into the front corner of the building where he knelt down behind a four-foot-high length of wall. He raised himself to peer through a gap. He couldn't see anyone, but he could hear movement near by.

Footfalls shuffled and then silenced, then shuffled again giving the impression that the men were hurrying along the backs of the buildings to the saloon.

Clumping footfalls echoed as two men hurried into the Lone Star followed by murmured comments when they found to their irritation that their quarry wasn't there.

'He can't have gone far,' someone said.

'Check out the front,' another man said from closer to. 'I'll scout around back there.'

'Wait!' a man at the front of the saloon said. 'I told you we were right to be cautious. We have been followed.'

A snorted laugh sounded. 'Now this sure is getting interesting.'

Everyone congregated in the saloon. A brief conversation took place in which the words were uttered too low for Tex to hear.

Then a man with a clipped tone spoke over the others, suggesting that orders were being delivered. This was followed by shuffling sounds as the men spread out around the saloon and got into positions where they could mount an assault on the newcomers.

Tex didn't know who the people in the saloon were, but their sneaky behaviour suggested they hadn't come to explain why he had been invited here, whereas the newer arrivals could have that aim in mind.

Presently the newcomers rode into his view. There were two men, one rangy and one massive. Tex didn't recognize them.

They were heading for the saloon side of the main drag at a steady, unconcerned pace that looked as if they didn't expect trouble. At the town sign they stopped, as Tex had done.

The rangy man looked along the road, taking in the abandoned buildings before he turned to the large man, who pointed to something on the ground, presumably Tex's tracks, and then to the saloon.

The first man nodded. Then they moved on. They

stopped outside the saloon.

The rangy man leaned forward in the saddle while the other man dismounted and stood with his bulging arms folded before the vacant eyes of the windows, appearing as if he were awaiting instructions.

'Elias Sutherland,' the mounted man called, 'are you in there?'

For long moments silence greeted him. Then movement sounded within the saloon and one of the earlier arrivals stomped to a halt in the doorway.

'Who are you?'

'Rafferty Horn and Bud.'

'Then I've got bad news for you, Rafferty. I'm Horatio Wilde. You've followed the wrong man.'

'I haven't. I was following you because I reckon you know what happened to Elias.'

Horatio didn't reply immediately and when he spoke his tone was low, giving Tex the impression he was lying.

'I've never heard of him.' Horatio moved forward. 'But you're welcome to look around town and see if you can find him.'

Tex frowned, seeing his intent. He was hoping to gather indirect aid in flushing him out, but luckily Rafferty shook his head.

'Obliged, but I've already confirmed what I thought.' Rafferty looked at Bud and inclined his head slightly. He lowered his voice. 'The stage did come here first.'

Horatio flinched, having gathered that Rafferty had relayed a message. He moved to raise a hand, but if he'd planned to convey a silent message of his own to the men inside, he didn't get to complete that message for, with surprising speed for a large man, Bud moved in.

Bud took a long pace forward, wrapped a huge hand around Horatio's upper arm, and swung him round while twisting his arm up his back so quickly and so far it made him yelp.

A moment later Horatio's face was mashed up against the saloon wall, the force of the collision being strong enough to rattle the wall and make Tex wonder if the building would cave in.

Rafferty watched the altercation with an amused smile on his lips, giving Tex the impression that he was familiar with this type of development. With untroubled movements he dismounted and walked on to stand beside the two men.

'Get him off me,' Horatio grunted, his breath coming in short gasps.

'You don't give the orders here. Get the other two men out here so I can question them.'

'Don't speak to me like that. There's three of us. We outnumber you.'

Rafferty shrugged. 'That won't help you none when Bud tears your arm off and strangles you with it.'

Bud raised his hand forcing his captive up on to his toes and making him bleat.

'Stop!' Horatio shouted, and when Bud didn't move, he looked at the window. 'Get out here!'

Two men hurried outside, encouraging Bud to lower his hand and let Horatio rock back down on to his heels. As Horatio uttered a sigh of relief, Bud swung him round to face the door.

The two men wore six-shooters at the hip and they were holding their hands low. They spread out showing that they were determined to win this stand-off if Bud harmed Horatio.

Bud and Rafferty didn't appear concerned that they faced superior numbers and Tex understood their confidence. It was clear that Horatio was the leader. And as Bud held him captive, that should give them a good chance of riding away from this confrontation.

'Now,' Rafferty said, resting a foot on the mouldering remnants of the hitching rail, 'I reckon it's time for us all to be honest with each other. The stage to Bear Creek was found abandoned outside town with one of its passengers missing. I want to know where he is.'

Horatio gulped. 'We don't know nothing about that.'

'You're lying. For some reason the stage passed through this ghost town before it rode into trouble. And now you're here. That's no coincidence.'

32

'If we ambushed the stage, why would we come here?'

'Perhaps you didn't find what you were looking for.'

Horatio didn't reply, his silence giving Tex the impression that Rafferty had stumbled across the truth.

Horatio's men must have realized this as they took long paces towards Rafferty, who appeared uncertain for the first time as he darted his gaze from left to right while backing away for a half-pace to keep them in view.

Tex reckoned he'd seen enough and, with his six-shooter thrust out, he stood.

'I reckon,' he called, 'you got that right, Rafferty.'

Everyone in the group started and then swirled round to face him. Rafferty was the first to respond.

'Who are you?' he asked.

'I'm Tex Callahan, the man they were looking for.'

CHAPTER 4

Rafferty Horn considered Tex Callahan. The startled reactions of the others said Tex wasn't in league with Horatio Wilde and the gun he'd aimed at his nearest antagonist said that he was siding with him.

'Do you know what happened to Elias, Tex?' he asked.

'No,' Tex said, 'but I'd like to know. I rode with him on the stage. I got left here and the stage moved on. That was the last I saw of him.'

Rafferty nodded, wondering how to continue asking questions without revealing that he knew only sketchy details of what Elias's business was, but Tex's response caused Horatio some concern. He shot a significant glance at the nearest man.

That man jerked round towards Tex with his hand moving quickly, but if he'd planned to go for his gun, he didn't get to complete the motion, for Tex reacted with instant and deadly force.

Gunfire exploded, sending the man twisting away with a hand rising to his bloodied chest above the heart. He keeled over without making a sound.

'No!' Horatio shouted, his voice desperate. Then he screeched in pain, the sound being cut off a moment before Tex's second shot hit the man to Rafferty's left high in the shoulder.

The man staggered sideways, clutching his wound, so Tex levelled his gun on him. He dispatched him with two rapid shots to the side. The man was still settling on the ground to lie sprawled on his back when Tex twirled his gun back in its holster.

During the few seconds while the gunfire had been erupting, Rafferty had only gathered enough of his wits to draw his gun, and he hadn't had the time to choose a target. He looked at Bud, who raised an eyebrow in surprise, this being the most animated activity he'd provided in a while.

Then Bud raised his hands from Horatio, who fell to his knees and then on to his chest with his neck bent at an angle that showed Bud had been hurried into killing him quickly.

Rafferty took a backward pace to consider the scene. He gulped to fight down the bile that burned his throat. The last time he'd visited Diamond Springs had been two years ago. As on that occasion, blood had been spilled.

Unbidden, his gaze rose to the Lone Star saloon, the scene of his first failure two years ago. Then it moved on to the stables down the road, the scene of the more disastrous failure.

He shook his head to stop himself dwelling on a troubled past he couldn't change and turned his attention back to the new atrocity.

'I guess,' Rafferty said, 'we won't get any answers from these men now.'

Tex shrugged as he walked on to check on the first man.

'Answers can always be got; you just have to live for long enough to ask them.'

Rafferty joined Tex in checking on the gunmen. Bud didn't even look at the fallen man at his feet.

'These men failed to do that, but I'm not sure they were planning to shoot you. The first man moved his hand quickly, but not towards his gun.' Rafferty waited for Tex to respond, but he only frowned, acknowledging that he might have been right. 'So what do you reckon they were after?'

Tex walked away to rummage through Horatio's pockets. He was thorough, but he was also clearly giving himself time to think how he would answer.

'I don't know,' he said when he'd finished. 'I was asked to come here, but I don't know why yet. I got the impression Elias had a mission in mind, but he wasn't talkative.'

'And the other man on the stage?'

'He was so quiet I didn't even learn his name.'

'That probably means he wasn't coming to see

Creswell Washington.'

Tex tensed. 'I didn't know Creswell was involved in this. Do you work for him?'

'Yeah.'

Tex took a deep breath and then straightened his back.

'Then I'm still obliged that your intervention helped me, but you'll leave town now.'

Tex cast a glance at his gun although he kept it holstered.

Rafferty considered. Tex had quick reactions and he was deadly accurate, but he was kneeling in a posture that was slightly turned away from him. Bud was standing only a few feet behind him.

Bud gave the impression that he was slow to react and ponderous when he moved, but when given an order he could bat away any man as if he were a fly. Afterwards, they never had any fight left in them.

'Sorry, Tex,' Rafferty said, smiling. 'I'm obliged for your intervention too. But I'll go where I choose to go until I get those answers I want.'

The years Rafferty and Bud had worked together had let them build up an understanding. So Rafferty was able to flick a mere glance at Bud that ordered him to subdue Tex but not kill him.

An instant later Bud leaned forward and swiped a huge hand around, the palm aimed on a trajectory that would slap Tex about the side of the head. As the hand parted air, Tex kept looking at Rafferty, but then at the last moment he jerked his head to the side while throwing up a hand.

He caught Bud's wrist and then twisted as he rose to his feet, letting the arm's momentum help him to get up. He ended the motion with Bud's arm raised sideways and the wrist bent backward.

An uncharacteristic bleat of pain tore from Bud's lips as he glared at Tex, but Tex merely held on to his wrist one-handed and gave a warning shake of the head that told Bud a quick movement would break it.

When Rafferty got over the shock of seeing Bud neutralized so easily, he saw that, without him noticing it, Tex had drawn his gun with his free hand and had aimed the weapon at him.

With a twist of the wrist that made Bud whimper and lower himself to his knees, presumably to lessen the tension that Tex's unusual grip was providing, Tex directed Rafferty to raise his hands. Then he considered them both.

'As I said,' Tex said with calm confidence, as if he'd never doubted he could turn the tables on them, 'to get your answers, you need to live for long enough to ask them.'

'I get your meaning,' Rafferty said. He took a long pace backward. 'I'll leave you to enjoy Diamond Springs's hospitality in peace.'

'Obliged.' Tex opened his hand, freeing Bud, who rubbed his wrist ruefully, that being his only reaction to being bettered so casually. 'And when you get back to Bear Creek, I'd be even more obliged if you'd do one more thing for me.'

'Which is?' Rafferty said, smiling as he regained his composure.

Tex returned the smile. 'Tell Creswell Washington that Tex Callahan is waiting for him.'

CHAPTER 5

Horatio Wilde's body had nothing on it that provided any clues about what the group's mission had been, and neither had the other men.

A search of their horses didn't reveal anything either and so Tex Callahan dragged their bodies round to the back of the saloon. He shooed their horses away, but he kept Horatio's bay so that he could leave if he didn't receive a visitor who would explain why he'd been invited here.

He returned to stand at the front of the saloon by which time Rafferty and Bud had disappeared into the distance as they returned to Bear Creek.

Tex felt sure that the answers he needed would be in that town and that they'd involve Creswell Washington, but he was content to wait for him to come to him.

Courtesy of Horatio's group, he now had food, water and a horse, and he still had the rest of the diary to read. So as the sun lowered he sought answers there.

Quickly, he rekindled his interest in the search for the buried diamond that glowed like a star.

Every day, customers told the bartender George Milligan what they'd found. Every day that turned out to be nothing, but more people started to believe that one day soon they would find it.

By three-quarters of the way through the diary, Tex was finding it hard not to just skip to the end and find out what happened. Half of the town was now on a mission to find the jewel while the other half looked on eagerly.

Only George, with his jaundiced comments, didn't believe anything would be found.

The source of the information on the whereabouts of the Lone Star was an old map that Loudon Sutherland now owned.

The name made Tex raise an intrigued eyebrow before he resumed reading about how Loudon sought help from his two brothers, who were knowledgeable local men.

Apparently, the map was water-damaged and so was hard to decipher. And so every day brought a new theory about its secrets and a new failure.

Four pages later came success.

Tex had become so taken up with everyone's lives that he grinned as he imagined their delight. He had to rely on his imagination to picture the scene, as

41

these diary entries were short, scrawled and probably penned when the writer was drunk.

The few sentences that related each day's events told of day-long parties and drunken revelry. It took a week for the accounts to become detailed again; then they described the sobering reality of a situation that was set to turn ugly.

Loudon and his brothers had directed the search. So they decided to split their windfall between them, but their good fortune attracted the interest of a newcomer to the area, Creswell Washington, who arrived with threats and the gunslinger Mitch Sawyer to back him up.

Tex broke off from reading to mutter to himself, having now understood the reason why he'd been hired. He and Creswell had met before.

Two years ago, Creswell had hired him to drive away homesteaders who had stood in his way. The money had been good, but Tex had hated knocking down people who were already at their lowest ebb.

He had refused to do Creswell's bidding. Then, in front of him, he'd set fire to his money and stamped the burnt paper into the dirt.

Then he'd walked away. But it hadn't helped the homesteaders. Creswell hired Mitch to shoot them up.

With only a few pages left in the diary, a confrontation between Loudon and Creswell was inevitable, but when Tex started reading again, it came sooner than he expected. When he turned over the page, a single entry reported the shocking result.

'Last night Creswell came,' Tex said, reading aloud. 'Loudon died, but he didn't talk, so Creswell didn't get the Lone Star. Nobody did.'

Tex turned over the page to find that the remaining pages were blank, although when he spread out the book to reveal the spine he saw that several pages had been torn out.

With the story ending abruptly, Tex assumed that afterwards the repercussions had destroyed the town. So now all that remained was the abandoned shells of buildings along with memories, but those memories were of a glittering star and they would never die.

Now, two years later, he had found this diary that someone had left for him to read. That meant that this someone had an idea about where the Lone Star was.

With nothing left for him to learn here, Tex slammed the diary shut. He tucked it in his pocket and headed outside to his horse.

The tracks told their story. The stage had stopped at the entrance to Devil's Canyon.

Rafferty had followed the stage's wheel ruts away from Diamond Springs, picking them up easily in the soft dirt. The tracks made by the three men who had been killed went in two directions.

Three miles from the place where the stage had been found abandoned, those tracks veered away to Devil's Canyon. In the shadow of a tangle of boulders, Rafferty found the place where it had stopped for a while.

Beyond, the tracks had been removed, but around one spot there were at least ten individual horse tracks. He found no discarded shell casings or dark patches of blood to suggest Elias's kidnapping had involved a fierce fight, or even that there had been an ambush at all, but beyond the boulders Bud made a grim discovery.

A shallow grave revealed the bloodied body of a man. The dead man had suffered a disfiguring facial gunshot wound and so, as Rafferty had seen Elias only briefly two years ago, he wasn't sure that it was him.

If it was Elias, the news would annoy Creswell, so Rafferty and Bud searched further afield, but they found nothing of interest.

With the sun about to set, Rafferty accepted that he'd learnt everything he could here today. So Bud draped the body over the back of his horse and they made their way back to Bear Creek.

When they arrived in town, the body gathered the kind of attention Rafferty had expected and an animated crowd was surrounding them when they stopped outside the sheriff's office. As he waited to report to Sheriff Bryce, Rafferty didn't join in the

44

developing discussions about the gruesome find.

He didn't have to wait long for the lawman to arrive and Bryce didn't wait long before he ushered him inside while beckoning Haywood to fetch the undertaker. Bud stayed outside and by the time Bryce was sitting behind a desk, his formidable presence had encouraged the onlookers to disband.

Using a neutral tone that acknowledged the sheriff's poor opinion of him, Rafferty explained about the situation out at Devil's Canyon.

'I'm obliged you've helped move this mystery on,' Bryce said when Rafferty had finished. 'But you shouldn't be looking for answers. I take care of the law, not Creswell Washington.'

'Creswell agrees, but you should accept he's concerned about the fate of his business associate.'

'I'll accept Creswell's concerns only on the day he's behind bars and you're in the cell next to him.'

Rafferty couldn't think of an answer to this attitude, so he looked past Bryce to the cells at the back of the law office. The only prisoner was the man who had been the sole occupant of the stage. He was lying on his back looking up at the ceiling and, first to Rafferty's surprise and then interest, he recognized him.

'Has George Milligan talked yet?'

'That's got nothing to do with Creswell,' Bryce snapped, although the brief flicker of his eyes showed that Rafferty's correct identification had interested him. He masked his concern by standing and going to the window.

'I'm not interested for Creswell's benefit,' Rafferty said to Bryce's back. 'I'm asking for mine.'

Bryce swirled round, his upper lip curled with contempt.

'On the day you went to work for Creswell, I might still have indulged you, but these days your interest worries me more than Creswell's.'

Rafferty cleared his throat and put on the most honest sounding tone he could manage.

'I've not lost my soul to Creswell. The man who used to work for you is still in here somewhere, fighting to get out.'

Bryce looked him up and down, his mouth opening to say something that the cold eyes said would be caustic, but then he dismissed him with a contemptuous wave and turned back to the window.

Silently, Bryce watched proceedings outside and when Rafferty moved to the door, he saw the problem that had drawn the sheriff's interest.

Creswell Washington had arrived and his gunslinger Mitch Sawyer was at his shoulder. Creswell was considering the body while the undertaker stood back. Then he quizzed Bud, who thought about his answer before uttering several words that made Creswell nod.

Despite the situation, Rafferty smiled, wondering how the taciturn Bud had summed up the situation so quickly.

Creswell then turned away from Bud to open the door of law office. He stood in the doorway, but he didn't enter, presumably to avoid the indignity of being rebuffed.

'Why are you wasting your time on that man, Bryce?' he asked.

'Because,' Bryce said, 'I've got a good idea who shot up Loudon Sutherland's brother.'

Bryce heaved a contented sigh. Then he gestured to Creswell to move aside so he could leave, but Creswell stood his ground.

'You know nothing, Bryce.' Creswell flashed a smile. 'That man isn't Elias Sutherland.'

For several seconds Bryce stayed looking at him, clearly weighing up whether he could trust him. Then he gave a brief nod and Creswell turned away. Rafferty and Bryce followed.

Out on the boardwalk, Bryce talked with Deputy Haywood, so, with the lawmen studiously ignoring them, Rafferty slipped in between Creswell and Mitch and they headed down the road to the Dark Night saloon. Bud lumbered along behind them.

'That true?' Rafferty asked when they'd moved out of the lawmen's hearing.

'Sure,' Creswell said. 'So who do you reckon the dead man is now?'

'One of the men who took Elias, I'd guess.' Rafferty shrugged. 'Although, aside from the dead

47

man, I didn't find any evidence of a fight.'

'There wouldn't be, and you're a long way from finding him. The dead man is the stage driver. He was working for me.'

Rafferty winced. He considered whether this was an appropriate time to question Creswell, but he judged that there never would be a good time.

'In which case it'd speed up my investigation if you told me the rest.'

Creswell stomped to a halt. With narrowed eyes, he stared down the boardwalk confirming that he viewed such questioning as showing defiance.

'The information I gave you is everything an employee of mine needs to know.'

'Even if that includes information about Tex Callahan?'

Creswell swirled round to face him with his eyes blazing. A moment later Mitch grabbed Rafferty's collar and pushed him back against the wall, scattering two passers-by and making them scurry away.

'What do you know about Tex?' Creswell demanded as Mitch drew him closer only to slam him back against the wall again.

Over Mitch's shoulder, Rafferty noted that Bud was considering the altercation with his usual blank gaze.

'Tex was on the stage with Elias,' Rafferty said. 'Now he's in Diamond Springs, where he shot up some men.'

Creswell looked him in the eye. 'Why did he get off the stage there, of all places?'

'I don't know that either and I didn't feel inclined to stay around to question him when he started shooting.'

Creswell snarled with irritation, then glanced at Mitch, who threw him aside.

'I should never have trusted you with such an important task.'

Previously, Rafferty would have been delighted to be given other duties, but this slight on his abilities made his blood pound in anger.

'I can do this,' he snapped with a level of venom that surprised him, 'even when you tie my hands behind my back with your half-truths.'

Creswell considered him with a calmness that was more troubling than his previous anger, causing Rafferty's own anger to leak away and making him wish he'd not spoken in haste. Creswell walked up to him.

'I shouldn't have doubted you,' he whispered. His hooded eyes hinted that despite his words good news wasn't forthcoming. 'I know what your anger can accomplish when you unleash it. After all, that was how you came to work for me, wasn't it?'

'I can never forget that,' Rafferty said with a catch in his throat.

'Then don't, because I'll trust you to find out what Tex wants and to bring me Elias.'

'Obliged,' Rafferty murmured.

Creswell laid a heavy hand on Rafferty's shoulder and squeezed.

'Do that and nobody ever need know that it was you who killed Loudon Sutherland in Diamond Springs.'

CHAPTER 6

For the last ten minutes the men in the camp had been talking.

Yesterday, Tex had followed tracks until the darkness had stopped his search. He'd picked them up again at first light.

Tex was a seasoned manhunter and he had easily distinguished Rafferty's and Bud's prints from the others. He'd followed these to an opened shallow grave. Then, using his experience, he'd found their campsite beside the river that emerged from Devil's Canyon and then circled round to the north of Bear Creek.

Tex had left Horatio's horse upriver and then made his way along the riverside, taking cover behind logs that had been washed up and anything else that was available. He had got to within a hundred yards of the group before concealing himself behind a mound where he was close enough

51

to watch them but not to hear what they were saying.

Not that he needed to hear them to know what was on their minds, as every few minutes someone looked up to see if anyone, presumably Horatio Wilde, was coming.

Their debate ended when one man moved on to stand by the river leaving the others to lean back against their saddles. Then he walked along the edge of the water while craning his neck to look upriver towards the direction Horatio would be coming, if he were able to.

As the man came closer Tex slipped down to lie below the top of the mound, where he awaited developments. The man's shadow edged forward into his view, then it stopped with him just feet away from a position where each would be able to see the other.

Tex quietly drew his gun and aimed it at the point where the man himself would come into sight if he moved forward. Patiently he waited, but the shadow remained still and when long minutes had passed, a feeling that something was wrong overcame him.

A shadow flittered at the edge of his vision and grit crunched.

Tex rolled over on to his side. Two men were crawling towards him through the scrub, coming from the opposite direction to the camp. Both men had drawn guns, which they swung up to aim at him, but Tex made them pay for their failure to sneak up on him unseen.

He slammed lead into the right-hand man's chest, making him drop without a sound. The second man had enough time to flatten himself to the ground, seeking the available low cover, but that didn't save him from Tex's accurate and deadly shot to the forehead.

Beyond the logs behind which Tex had hidden earlier another gunman scurried into view, with his head down before he went to ground. Then the man by the river also moved into view with his gun drawn.

Tex swung round to him, but mindful of what had happened in Diamond Springs he stilled his fire; and he was glad he had done so when the man blasted lead into the scrub ten feet away from the two attackers. A screech sounded and a man rose into view, clutching his shoulder, only for Tex to dispatch him with a shot that tore into his chest.

As Tex acknowledged his helper, that man was joined by a second man from the camp, Elias Sutherland.

'You're not supposed to be here, Tex,' Elias called. He went on to identify the other man as his brother Brewster.

Tex nodded to them. 'You should be pleased that I am.'

Elias smiled as the other men from the camp joined them and spread out on both sides of the mound. Everyone took up positions facing the logs with their guns drawn. Brewster and Elias slipped into position beside him.

'Why did you leave Diamond Springs?' Elias asked. 'I sent Horatio Wilde there to make sure you waited for Creswell Washington to take the bait.'

Tex winced. Unfortunately, Rafferty had been right in saying Horatio hadn't come to shoot him up. He had reacted too quickly and now three men lay dead, a fact that these men must never discover.

He weighed up his options. Despite them appearing to have a common enemy, the truth could leave him dead. Then again, a lie could lead to the same result. He took a deep breath.

'I'm sorry to tell you this,' he said. 'Horatio got shot up.'

'Who did it?' Elias snapped.

'I don't know.' Tex met Elias's eye. 'But in my experience, when Creswell is involved men tend to die.'

'Men who work for Creswell aren't enjoying themselves no more.' Elias looked upriver and blasted off a speculative shot at the man behind the logs. 'Did you find the grave at Devil's Canyon?'

'Sure. Except it was empty.'

Elias grunted with irritation. 'That was the stage driver's. I didn't tell you about my plans because I'd figured out he'd been paid to make sure I ended up in Creswell's hands. He failed, but as that means Creswell knows of my plans, I sent George Milligan to Bear Creek in my place.'

As Elias smiled at having named George, their assailant blasted off a gunshot that pounded into the mound between two men, encouraging Elias's men to pepper lead at the log. Then they all shuffled backward to seek better cover behind the mound.

Tex stilled his fire and rested his gun on the mound as he awaited a chance for a clear shot.

'I read his diary,' he said. 'It told an interesting story.'

Elias nodded. 'George was our silent companion on the stage. He'll now be under the protection of Bear Creek's unknowing lawmen.'

With quick gestures, as if to emphasize the urgency of their situation, Elias pointed to each man in turn and named them.

Tex smiled. He had come across some of the names before when he had read in the diary about the colourful characters who had frequented the Lone Star saloon.

'You're all from Diamond Springs?' he said.

'Sure,' Elias said. 'We were there when Diamond Springs died. And now we're back to claim the Lone Star and make our town live again.'

'In that case, tell me where it is so I can start planning.'

'Its fate is no concern of yours, but I can tell you this: George worked it out after re-reading his own diary.'

'Then I have bad news for you.' Tex withdrew the

diary from his pocket and slapped it down on the top of the mound. He drew Elias's attention to the missing pages. 'Someone tore out the final sheets. I'd guess the answer was there.'

Elias bunched a fist. 'I hadn't noticed it'd been damaged. We'll have to hope that Creswell doesn't have the missing pages.'

'If he has, he'll now have the Lone Star. Creswell doesn't waste time.'

'And that means neither can you.'

'If you insist . . .' Tex murmured, while noting that the man behind the log was edging up to take another shot at them. Before he could fire Tex scythed a deadly shot into the gunman's neck that stood him upright before he toppled from view.

As Elias's men whooped with delight, Elias pointed towards Bear Creek.

'With Creswell's first attempt to take us on dealt with, it's time for you to carry out your mission.'

'Which is?' Tex asked, although he'd already figured out the answer.

'Kill Creswell Washington.'

'It's a pity you didn't tell me that straight away.' Tex smiled as he holstered his gun. 'For such a mission, you wouldn't have had to pay me a dime.'

CHAPTER 7

Bud was late.

Rafferty's silent companion was usually punctual so this only added to Rafferty's sense of foreboding that today would turn out to be a bad day.

Rafferty walked his horse back and forth outside the stables. After a few minutes he spotted Bud's large form ambling down the boardwalk towards him, but, to his irritation, coming in the opposite direction was Sheriff Bryce.

When the lawman was close enough for Rafferty to see that his expression was thunderous, he mounted up in case a quick retreat was required.

'Like you, I thought I'd head out to Devil's Canyon,' Bryce said when he arrived, 'but you being here saves me from making another journey.'

'We plan to look for anything we missed yesterday,' Rafferty said, speaking levelly while avoiding meeting Bryce's piercing gaze. 'We'll tell you what we find.'

'You may not have enough time.' Bryce waited for Rafferty to make the obvious retort. When he didn't, the lawman continued: 'Because I don't reckon you'll still be a free man come sundown.'

'I had nothing to do with what happened out there. I was collecting Creswell's debts when the stage was diverted.'

'I know you were and that's the problem.' Bryce narrowed his eyes. 'Oliver Lee was killed this morning. His neck was broken.'

Rafferty winced, his mind racing. 'The last time I saw Oliver was yesterday after he'd paid me the money he owed Creswell.'

He had told the truth, but he also knew that Creswell couldn't allow his defiance to go unpunished. Someone had to pay and as he was giving him leeway for now, the recipient of the stolen money was that man.

Bryce sneered, then glanced at the approaching Bud.

'And that's why I hate dealing with men like you and Creswell. I believe you, but it's a truth that hides a lie.' Bryce set his feet wide apart and moved his hand to his holster. Slowly he drew his gun, although he held it low. 'I've stood by for too long, so Oliver will be the last man to die at your and Creswell's hands. I'm taking him on now.'

Rafferty tried to meet Bryce's gaze, but he couldn't.

'You have proof?'

'Not of your and Creswell's involvement yet, of course. But Oliver was killed by a strong man who snapped his neck like a twig. I know of only one man who could do that.'

'Bud didn't do it,' Rafferty said with as much assurance as he could muster, even though he hadn't seen Bud since last night.

'This time I know what your guarded answer means. Bud is just a weapon that does the bidding of others. I can't get to the others, so for now I'll settle for disarming the weapon. If you want me to arrest him alive, order him to follow my instructions.'

Rafferty lowered his head while he considered his options, but other than making a run for it with Bud, he couldn't think of one. Bud was now stomping to a halt before them in his usual docile way, so Rafferty gestured to him.

'Bud, you need to go with the lawman,' he said. 'Don't give him any trouble and I'll work on getting you free.'

Bud's only reaction was the slight stiffening of his with which he often responded when given an order, as if this one was no different from his usual instructions.

'Obliged for that,' Bryce said. 'When I link you to Oliver's death, I hope you'll come quietly too.'

'If you uncover the truth behind the lies, you'll find that I had nothing to do with it.'

59

Bryce snorted as he directed Bud to leave by using a quick gesture with his gun.

'If only you'd met my eye when you said that, I might have believed you. The trouble is, you still have a scrap of decency left in you and that means that unlike Creswell you can feel guilty.'

Bryce gave Rafferty a long glare, then moved on with Bud walking a few paces ahead of him at gun-point.

As Rafferty watched them leave he sighed, noting that Bryce was making Bud's arrest an obvious one so that Creswell was sure to be informed.

'I'll uncover the truth,' he shouted after Bryce, 'no matter how uncomfortable that may be for me.'

Bryce didn't look back or even acknowledge him. But strangely, Bud looked over his shoulder and turned up the corners of his lips with an expression so rare for him that it took Rafferty a few seconds to realize he was smiling.

Now feeling even more disconcerted, Rafferty swung his horse away and headed out of town.

Rafferty knelt beside the shallow grave.

As he had failed to work out which direction the men who had killed the stage driver had taken when they'd left Devil's Canyon, his thoughts dwelt on his troubled past. For the past few hours his thoughts had been locked on that time since last night when he'd accepted that Elias's disappearance had to be connected to the events they had both witnessed.

He had also decided that when he found him he wouldn't do Creswell's bidding. Instead, he would help Elias.

For now, in his preoccupied state, he could easily imagine that the grave was the one situated outside Diamond Springs, so he moved away and sat down on a rock. He looked east towards the distant town that was on his mind, letting himself be taken back to that time.

Two years ago, he had been Sheriff Bryce's deputy in Bear Creek when the news had come in that trouble was brewing in Diamond Springs.

Bryce had reckoned that trouble had been brewing in Diamond Springs for far too long and he wasn't prepared to waste time travelling there and back. He had sent Rafferty instead.

When Rafferty rode into town a confrontation was in progress.

The fortunate – up until now – Loudon Sutherland and his two brothers Elias and Brewster had holed up in the Lone Star saloon, while Creswell Washington and his men had taken up covered positions on the boardwalk opposite. The rest of the townsfolk had scurried into hiding.

'The situation is under control,' Creswell said, 'so why has a deputy sheriff come here?'

Rafferty considered the saloon where one man was

at the window keeping watch. As Rafferty was taking his time to reply, Creswell's main gunslinger Mitch Sawyer stepped up to scowl at him, confirming Rafferty's fear that ending this siege without bloodshed would probably be impossible.

'To keep the situation that way,' Rafferty said, using a light tone that was at odds with how he felt. 'And so I'm pleased to meet you folk. If you want a friendly drink in the saloon, I'll arrange that. Otherwise, move on.'

'I'll move on,' Creswell said. He walked up to Rafferty to look him in the eye. 'But only when I have the Lone Star diamond. And so I'd be obliged if you'd apply the law and make Loudon Sutherland hand it over to its rightful owner.'

Creswell's anger had sounded sincere, so Rafferty moved backward a pace.

'I'll hear your side of the story,' he said. 'Then I'll hear Loudon's.'

Creswell nodded, although he cast a sly glance at the dozen or so men who were lined up along the boardwalk, suggesting he wouldn't accept Rafferty's judgement if it didn't favour him.

'Last month I had some trouble with homesteaders. One man was persuaded to pay me off with an old map.' Creswell paused when Mitch snorted a laugh. 'I was figuring out what it showed when Loudon Sutherland started working for me. He stole the map and ran.'

Creswell finished his story by gesturing angrily at the saloon.

'I'd heard he'd uncovered some information,' Rafferty said, 'but not that he stole it off you.'

Before Creswell could complain any more, Rafferty tipped his hat to Creswell and Mitch and moved on. He walked across the road to the saloon with his hands raised slightly.

By the time he was standing before the door, Creswell had scurried into hiding in an alley. Rafferty beckoned to the man who was looking through the window.

He received a welcoming wave, so he went in. The three brothers who were at the centre of this crisis had taken up positions around the room.

They introduced themselves. Aside from Elias at the window, Brewster was guarding a second door that presumably led out to the back.

Loudon was sitting at the bar nursing an untouched whiskey. He signalled that Rafferty should join him. The bartender was the only other man there and he was keeping his head down, his slouched posture suggesting he wished he were elsewhere.

'Obliged that the law has stepped in,' Loudon said. 'But I wanted Sheriff Bryce. He understands the situation.'

'He's busy, and besides he thought a fresh viewpoint might find a compromise.'

Loudon slammed a fist on the bar, his eyes narrowing with anger before he got himself under control with a shake of the shoulders.

'We're not interested in no compromise. We found the Lone Star. Creswell Washington isn't having it.' Loudon's brothers muttered their support along with making deprecating comments about Creswell that made Rafferty smile. 'And Creswell sure isn't interested in no compromise either.'

'I agree that's unlikely when he reckons he's in the right.'

Loudon winced and a silence dragged on for several seconds telling Rafferty everything he needed to know about Creswell's story.

'It's not like it seems,' Loudon said, his voice low. 'He probably stole the map in the first place and he had no idea what the notations meant. He'd never have found nothing if I hadn't worked out that it detailed an area near here and then we hadn't searched and dug up the diamond ourselves.'

Rafferty fixed him with his level gaze. 'In other words, you have less right to the Lone Star than he has.'

Loudon favoured him with a smile, acknowledging he'd made a valid point, but Brewster came over waving his arms in irritation.

'Sheriff Bryce should be here,' he snapped. 'He knows us. He wouldn't side with Creswell.'

'Perhaps he wouldn't,' Rafferty said, speaking

calmly, 'but I reckon he'd try to find a solution that would satisfy everyone.'

'Creswell wants the Lone Star,' Loudon said, fixing Rafferty with his honest gaze, 'and then Diamond Springs will die. These days people are leaving for Bear Creek, but we're planning to stay. We'll sell the diamond and use the money for the benefit of our town. We'll build us up to be better than Bear Creek could ever be. Creswell would never do anything like that.'

Rafferty spread his hands and lowered his voice to a more placatory tone.

'What would you do if you were me?'

'I'd be able to tell we're good men,' Loudon said immediately, 'and that we'd sooner die than let that man have what's ours.'

His brothers uttered supportive grunts, but Rafferty shook his head.

'Then you'll die, because no matter who's in the right here, I can't prevail against all of Creswell's men and neither can you. That means Creswell will get the Lone Star. The only hope is for you to offer a deal.'

For long moments nobody spoke. Instead, they cast worried glances at each other. Their slight nods and facial tics said that the brothers were having a silent debate that didn't need to be spoken aloud. It ended when Loudon stood and faced him, his full whiskey glass clutched to his chest.

'There's only one way we'll win through,' he whispered with a gulp, 'and that needs us to lose.'

Rafferty shook his head. 'If you want me to get involved in that plan, you'll have to stop speaking in riddles.'

Loudon swirled his glass, the action masking a tremor in his right hand.

'Then I'll make it plain. Leave town. Leave us to fight this out.'

'I can't do that. I'm a lawman. I have to stay.'

'I know and I guess that's why Bryce sent you instead of facing this situation himself,' Loudon said, his tone resigned. 'So if you won't leave, you may find that there's only one option. We want you to take it.'

'Which is?' Rafferty said, his voice low as he noticed everyone's sombre mood.

Loudon raised the whiskey glass to his lips and drained it in one gulp.

'Let me die,' he said.

CHAPTER 8

'I'll never stand by and let you get killed,' Rafferty said with a shocked gasp.

He wondered if Loudon had made a bad joke, but Loudon and his brothers returned his gaze levelly.

'I don't want you to, either,' Loudon said with a rueful smile. He withdrew a short broken match from his pocket, showing the process that had been used to reach the decision that had ended his lucky streak. 'But as a last resort, we reckon it's the only way to stop Creswell getting our diamond.'

Rafferty shook his head and set his hands on his hips.

'And how will your death accomplish that?'

Loudon looked around the room, gathering nods from both brothers.

'I've hidden the Lone Star somewhere where Creswell will never find it. If he takes me alive, he's sure to make me talk, but if I die, my secret dies with me.'

Rafferty shrugged, still incredulous that the brothers had seriously planned for this option.

'And then the Lone Star will be lost again, perhaps this time for ever.'

'It won't. I've given orders that'll avoid that possibility. As long as my brothers can escape, they can avenge me by killing Creswell later. Then my sacrifice won't be wasted.'

Loudon clamped his mouth tightly shut in an exaggerated way that told Rafferty not to endanger their ill-conceived plan by asking for more details.

Rafferty lowered his head, lost for words and, with nobody saying anything more, he turned to the door and made his slow way across the saloon room. At the door he stopped and looked back, meeting the gaze of each man in turn.

They all returned expressions that were a mixture of defiance and despair, and despite his determination to find an alternative course of action, Rafferty couldn't help but think they'd already given up.

He went outside on to the boardwalk with his hands raised. He gestured for calm and received a beckoning wave from Creswell. Rafferty joined him in the alley facing the saloon. Creswell wasted no time before he demanded answers.

'When is Loudon handing over my diamond?' he said.

'Never.' Rafferty waited until Creswell clenched a fist in anger. Then he shot a narrow-eyed glare at

Mitch before he continued. 'And if you kill him, you'll still not get the diamond. He's hidden it. Even his brothers don't know where.'

'Obliged for the advice.' Creswell rubbed his jaw while catching Mitch's eye.

'That's not advice. I'm here to—'

Mitch's shadow flickered on the ground alerting Rafferty and making him turn, but he reacted too slowly. Mitch's double-handed punch thudded into the back of his neck and sent him reeling away until his forehead slammed against the wall with a sickening thud.

He keeled over and lay for several moments. Then he slapped his hands to the ground and tried to force himself upright, but his limbs wouldn't obey him.

He flopped back down. Then all he could do was listen to Creswell's assault on the Lone Star saloon in fragmented bursts as he flitted in and out of consciousness.

Gunfire and cries of alarm burst out. Rapid footfalls sounded. Then the commotion became quieter as the battle receded from him, but whether that was as a result of his disorientated state or because it had happened in reality he couldn't tell.

A sudden explosion of distant gunfire brought him back to full consciousness. But when he opened his eyes and rolled over on to his side he found that he must have blanked out for a longer stretch than he'd thought, as he was alone.

He clambered to his feet groggily and, with a determined tread to overcome the pounding in his head, he set off for the saloon. His gait became uncertain and before he reached the saloon his strength gave way, so he veered away to grab hold of the hitching rail, where he stood swaying.

Raised voices sounded, seemingly coming from some distance away, but in his befuddled state he doubted he could do anything to help Loudon Sutherland.

He set off anyhow.

He reached the saloon wall and then walked himself along to the door. He peered inside. Nobody was there.

He was about to manoeuvre himself inside when a burst of gunfire tore out from down the road. The gunfight had clearly moved on from the saloon, but Rafferty consoled himself with the thought that at least this meant Loudon and his brothers were still alive.

He rolled his shoulders and gathered his strength. Then he moved off towards the sound of gunfire. He managed three uncertain paces and was planning on how he'd move off the boardwalk when he stumbled.

With a frantic waving of the arms he tried to keep his footing, but he failed and fell with his arms thrust out.

To his surprise he didn't hit the ground. Instead,

he stopped in mid-air. Then he rose up and glided along beside the saloon.

He closed his eyes, hoping to overcome his giddiness, but when he opened his eyes, he was still gliding through the air.

He presumed he'd fallen unconscious and he was now dreaming. So he enjoyed his serene state until a gust of cold wind cooled his face and helped him to gather enough of his wits to realize what had happened.

Someone had caught him before he could hit the ground and now he was being carried down the road tucked under an arm. He craned his neck and looked up into the craggy face of a large man, who was holding him up without making any obvious exertion.

'Obliged,' he said.

'Bud,' his saviour said. He resumed looking straight ahead.

Rafferty fought to banish his disorientated feeling and to get his thoughts in order; that helped him to remember that he'd been told that Bud was one of the men Loudon had employed to find the Lone Star. He might even have been the one who had made the actual discovery.

Bud walked on until he reached the last group of buildings on the edge of the town. Creswell Washington was standing back in a safe position while his men had taken up positions around the stables in the same manner as that in which they had previously surrounded the saloon.

After a few moments they fired through the doorway. When the men inside failed to return gunfire the attackers edged forward to closer positions while covering each other.

Bud dismissed this battle with a determined swing of the body and he moved off towards the building behind the stables, taking Rafferty and himself away from the gunfight.

The sounds of the battle receded, but Rafferty conserved his strength until they reached the building, where he was raised upright and propped up against the wall.

'I'm feeling well enough to help Loudon now,' Rafferty said after gathering his breath.

Bud looked him over, presumably taking in the fact that he was holding on to the wall to keep himself upright. He shook his head.

'I help,' he said.

Rafferty conceded with a nod that Bud would have to take the lead.

'What are you going to do?'

'Follow orders.'

Bud turned away to face the doorway. He stood with his hands on his hips, as if he expected something to happen.

Sure enough, after another burst of gunfire at the front of the stables, Rafferty heard feet scurrying inside the building.

Then the besieged brothers emerged through the doorway, having presumably taken a secret route from the stables. They took in the sight of Bud and then bunched up. They had paid a painful price for their defiance.

All three men were bloodied. Elias was hobbling and he was holding up Brewster whose slack expression made him appear oblivious to what was happening.

'Let's get you to somewhere safe,' Rafferty said, beckoning with a weak gesture.

Loudon considered him. 'You seem to be in as bad a state as we are.'

'I am.' Rafferty looked down the road to the front of the stables, where consternation was growing, presumably as Creswell's men discovered that the brothers were no longer inside. 'But that doesn't mean we can't avoid further bloodshed.'

'There's only one way we can do that.' Loudon cast a long look at Elias before he faced Bud. He took a deep breath and then lowered his voice. 'You have your orders.'

Bud nodded. When he moved towards him, Loudon underhanded his gun to him.

Rafferty assumed Bud was going to cover them while they sought a safe place to hole up. As he was too weak to help with that defence, he turned, aiming to join them in retreating.

Then Loudon's instruction reminded him of their last conversation in the saloon.

With a shocked hollowness in his stomach, he swirled round, but a burst of nausea made him sway. By the time he'd righted himself, he was too late.

Bud was already carrying out his order.

Rapid gunfire blasted out as Bud's gun tore lead into Loudon's chest. Loudon went down without making a sound.

For long moments Rafferty could do nothing but lean back against the wall and watch the gunsmoke swirl. Only when Bud lowered his gun did he break out of his fugue and move on to join him.

'You didn't have to carry out that order,' Rafferty murmured, lost for anything else to say.

Bud turned and considered him.

'Why?' he said simply, as if Rafferty had suggested the most difficult concept he'd ever encountered.

While meeting Bud's blank gaze, Rafferty removed the gun from his huge hand. Bud didn't complain, so he moved on to check on Loudon. He was dead, his secret preserved.

The shock of confirming he'd enacted his bizarre sacrifice made Rafferty stand back, shaking his head. By the time Creswell arrived, Elias had dragged Brewster away into the shadows and Rafferty was still standing dumbfounded with Bud at his side.

Creswell appraised the scene with much nodding before he patted his back.

'You did the right thing there,' he said, 'in the end.'

'I?' Rafferty murmured.

'Sure.' Creswell winked. 'I didn't think a lawman would have the guts to do it, but you shot up the right man.'

Rafferty looked down at the still smoking gun in his hand, now realizing how this situation must look.

'This doesn't mean I sided with you,' he said.

'But it does,' Creswell said with a grin. 'And that means that from this day forward, you're mine.'

And he was. And so was Bud.

That night, Loudon's sacrifice bought the surviving brothers the time they needed to get away from town. But, over the next few weeks, Creswell couldn't accept that he would never find the Lone Star. The mayhem he caused while searching for it drove other townsfolk away. That started a rot that spread until the town died.

No matter what Creswell did, Rafferty couldn't stop him as Creswell had a hold over him, even if that hold was different from the one Creswell thought he had.

Creswell reckoned he'd killed Loudon Sutherland, whereas Rafferty knew that Bud had followed Loudon's orders. That meant Bud didn't deserve to be punished, but as Rafferty reckoned nobody would believe the actual version of events, he couldn't talk about Bud's role. So, officially,

75

Loudon's death became an unsolved mystery.

Over the next few months Creswell took control of Rafferty's life. Before long he had resigned as deputy sheriff and started working for Creswell while Bud worked for Rafferty.

As best as he was able, Rafferty kept Bud in line and ensured he always gave him orders that fell short of the worst that a man who never questioned his duties could do.

So it was that their odd relationship had started. It was one that was still controlled by the events of two years ago.

So when, with those events relived, Rafferty shook the bad memories away, he still felt as tired as he had done when he'd stood over Loudon's body with a gun in hand and Creswell leering at him.

With his back bowed he trudged off. He planned to head back to his horse and then scout around in search of tracks to follow. He came out from behind the rocks, then slid to a halt. Sheriff Bryce was waiting for him.

'I said you wouldn't still be free by sundown,' Bryce said. 'Rafferty Horn, you're under arrest.'

'I want to see George Milligan,' Tex said.

Deputy Haywood shook his head and moved out from behind his desk to bar Tex's way.

'I'm sorry,' he said. 'Sheriff Bryce's orders are that

nobody's allowed to see him, and he's not in town to change that ruling.'

Tex frowned, making it appear that he was debating his next move. In truth, he had waited until he'd seen Bryce leave town before he'd come to the law office.

His instincts had told him to follow up the clues in George's diary first, although he was also as interested as everyone else was to know what had happened to the Lone Star.

'But I reckon he's innocent. I was with him on the stage before Elias went missing. He's not the kind of man who'd be involved with that.'

'Really?' Haywood said, his lip curled with scepticism. When Tex kept his expression placid, the deputy appeared to get over his suspicions and sighed. 'You can have one minute with him, but if you try anything, you'll join him in his cell.'

Haywood gestured for him to join him in approaching the cells, so Tex moved on. George was lying on his cot and not looking at him.

The only other prisoner was a huge man in the adjoining cell. He was standing solidly at the cell door. His massive hands, which were clutching two bars, looked as if they could demolish the cell if he chose to.

'Bud?' Tex said. The prisoner didn't react, but when Haywood flinched back with surprise, Tex turned to him. 'I met him recently. He sure got himself into trouble quickly.'

'He killed a man. Bryce has gone to arrest his accomplice.'

'Would that be Creswell Washington?'

'You know plenty for a man who just rode into town.'

Haywood raised an eyebrow, but when Tex didn't take the opportunity to explain, he stepped back, leaving Tex to talk with George, although he stayed close enough to hear their conversation.

Tex stepped up to the cell door, his footfalls making George sit up on his cot and look at him. He smiled briefly, making Tex hope that he'd overheard enough to know who he was.

'What do you want?' George asked levelly.

'To help you,' Tex said. 'Do you need anything?'

George stood up. He paced his cell twice, his furrowed brow showing that he was trying to find a way to help him without alerting the deputy.

'I'll rest easier knowing my property is safe.' George came up to the bars to address Haywood. 'Let him have my possessions.' He nodded towards Tex.

Haywood narrowed his eyes and looked from one man to the other. With a shake of the head he appeared to dismiss the possibility that they had sneaked information past him.

He went to his desk and extracted a box from which he took out a folded bundle containing several

78

dollars, a watch and other small items. Haywood detailed them before handing them over.

Tex kept his expression blank so as not to draw attention to the only item that interested him: four folded-over pages with rough edges that looked as if they'd been torn from the diary.

When Haywood had handed over everything, Tex tucked the items in a pocket and promised to return later if he learnt anything useful. He didn't look at the cells again and left the office.

Out on the boardwalk, he looked for somewhere quiet to read the pages. The Dark Night saloon was to his left and so he went right, heading to the stables.

It was late afternoon and few people were about, so he was beginning to wonder whether he should just stop and read the full story while leaning on a convenient wall when four men walked out of an alley ahead.

They spread out across the boardwalk to block his way in an organized manner that suggested they'd been waiting for him.

Tex put the diary from his mind and stopped to consider them. They all returned his gaze neutrally waiting for him to make the first move. As his horse was in the stables beyond them, he had no choice but to move on.

He still waited and after a few moments the men spread out to leave room for Creswell Washington to come out of the alley and stand with two men flanking him on either side.

Tex and Creswell faced each other, their firm gazes acknowledging that after their last encounter neither man had wanted to see the other again, but now that they had they would resolve their unfinished business.

'It's good to see you, Creswell,' Tex said, speaking in what he hoped sounded like a disconcertingly civil manner.

Creswell sneered before his gaze flicked past Tex's shoulder. Too late Tex realized the full extent of the trap he'd walked into.

He swivelled round on a heel to find that Mitch Sawyer had followed him after he'd left the law office. He was standing in the centre of the boardwalk with his right hand dangling beside his holster.

'I reckon,' Mitch said with a sly grin, 'it's time for you to apologize to Creswell.'

CHAPTER 9

'I'll hear that apology in my office,' Creswell said, pointing down the boardwalk to the Dark Night saloon.

Tex considered him and then Mitch Sawyer, who moved past him to stand at Creswell's shoulder. Seeing that he had no choice, he led the way to Creswell's saloon.

As it was late afternoon, the saloon room was only half-full, but a steady stream of customers was arriving. They all wisely gave Creswell's group a wide berth and avoided catching anyone's eye.

Creswell signified that they should head up the stairs, but Tex shook his head and picked a circular table in the corner.

'I'd like to leave when I choose to,' he said.

Creswell muttered something under his breath, but Tex walked on and sat down with his back to the wall.

Creswell and Mitch joined him, sitting at the table to his right and left. The other men stood beside the nearest table until its patrons decided they were needed elsewhere. Then they sat and watched them.

'You lost that option,' Creswell said, leaning on the table, 'when you rode into my town.'

'You said that the last time we met. But that day you were the one who got lucky.'

Creswell firmed his jaw before speaking; only a slight narrowing of his eyes showed that he was irritated.

'I was. Your defiance meant I looked elsewhere. I found Mitch.' He gestured to Mitch, who responded with a mocking tip of the hat. 'That's worked out fine. He's a faster draw than you are and he does what I tell him to.'

Creswell raised an eyebrow, inviting Tex to insult him again and test that claim.

'Mitch is no threat to me. He couldn't even complete your simple mission to intercept the stage.' Tex smiled when Mitch's right eye twitched, confirming that his assumption had been right. 'But quit the pleasantries, Creswell. I'm not apologizing, so say what's on your mind.'

Creswell nodded and leaned back in his chair.

'Are you working for Elias Sutherland?'

'I am.' Tex smiled. 'And I'm not the only one, as the first group of men you sent after him found out.'

'If that was meant to worry me, it failed. I knew

82

others were helping him when he avoided his fate.' Creswell waved a dismissive hand. 'But that's no problem. Mitch can kill him later.'

When Creswell's indirect show of support, despite his recent failure, made Mitch nod approvingly, Tex couldn't help but laugh before he matched Creswell's posture by leaning back in his chair.

'Don't waste your breath, Creswell. I once worked for you. I know that when you're worried, you raise the stakes with bluster and bravado.'

'Except I'm not blustering. I know about the diary in Diamond Springs.' Creswell smiled and spread his hands in a benevolent gesture. 'Although I'll admit I do enjoy raising the stakes, but only when I know I can win.'

A discarded pack of cards was on the table; the last winning hand was still lying face up with the rest of the cards sitting where they'd fallen. With his gaze set on Tex, Creswell gathered up the cards, shuffled casually, and then dealt them both five cards.

Tex fingered his face-down cards, but when Creswell picked his up, he changed his mind and left them where they lay without looking at them.

'What are we playing for?' he asked, folding his arms.

'The Lone Star,' Creswell said.

'It's not mine to give, and besides, why do you reckon I know where it is?'

'I know you don't have that information because I

have it.' Creswell tapped his cards on the table. 'So if I win, I'll keep the Lone Star. If you win, I'll show you to it.'

Tex nodded. 'In that case I'll play these cards.'

Creswell licked his lips, as if he'd expected this response. He discarded and dealt himself three cards. He shuffled his collection and then considered Tex over the top of them.

Tex beckoned Creswell to show his hand first. Cresswell revealed two threes. Then, with his gaze set on Creswell, Tex turned over his cards one at a time.

Creswell didn't look at the cards, so Tex glanced down. He had three aces, an unlikely hand on a straight draw.

'Seems you're a lucky man today,' Creswell said calmly.

'So show me the Lone Star,' Tex said, seeing no possible action other than to play out Creswell's ruse to its conclusion. He smiled. 'I'd guess it's in your office.'

'You're not only a lucky man, you're a perceptive man.'

Tex stood up and gestured, signifying that Creswell should lead on, which he did without complaint while Mitch and the other men filed up behind him. They trailed across the saloon room with the customers avoiding looking their way.

At the bottom of the stairs, Creswell gathered the other men around him. He whispered quick instructions, which Tex couldn't hear, making them smile and then head away to the door. As they slipped outside, Creswell and Mitch climbed slowly while, climbing between them. Tex looked out for trouble.

The corridor at the top of the stairs was empty with one door on the right and two doors on the left. Creswell stopped beside the door to the right. He pushed it open, but he made no move to enter.

At Tex's back, Mitch was close enough for him to hear his breathing and Creswell had a contented gleam in his eye. Tex couldn't hear any sounds coming from within the office, but it was likely that someone was waiting for him to enter.

'And what you want me to see is in there?' he said, playing for time.

Creswell nodded, although he also smirked, so Tex waited for long enough to let anyone who was inside get agitated. Then he jerked forward to glance through the doorway before moving back.

In his short perusal he had confirmed that the large office was empty, so he smiled at Creswell, receiving a knowing smile in return. Then he moved on.

He decided that if Creswell was the first to follow him through the doorway he would grab him and then hold him at gunpoint. But, as it turned out, Mitch followed him, a move that confirmed to Tex that he was to be killed in here.

Tex moved quickly. He grabbed the edge of the

door and while leaping to the side, he hurled the door backwards into Mitch's face. The door collided with his body with a satisfying thud before it flung him out into the corridor.

A table was to the side of the door. With only moments to make a barrier, Tex grabbed the legs, tipped it on its side, and dragged it across the doorway.

The table turned out to be heavier than it looked and he had to strain to reach the door, by which time Creswell and Mitch were pushing the door open. The door had opened for a foot when the tabletop slid into the doorway and made the door shudder to a halt.

He carried on with his effort and drew the table all the way across the doorway. Then he pressed it back against the wall to close the door.

He judged that the table was heavy enough to hold for a while. More important, as the door was the only entrance, he should be able to survive a siege.

He hurried across the office to Creswell's desk. He knelt down behind the desk and, with his gun hand held steady on the top, he aimed at the door and waited for someone to make the mistake of breaking in.

'That was a big mistake,' Creswell said from the corridor. 'I really had only planned to show you the Lone Star.'

'Of course you had,' Tex said. 'So you'll be pleased

to know I'm looking for it right now.'

He pushed several books and a lamp off the desk to emphasize his point.

'You won't find it without my help and even if you do, you're trapped in there.'

Creswell didn't sound concerned and Tex's actions ought to have annoyed him. That meant Creswell still reckoned he was in control and, worse, in some way he had played into his hands.

When long minutes had passed without him hearing any movement in the corridor, Tex looked around the room, wondering where he should search for whatever Creswell had really brought him here to see.

Several cupboards and a safe were against the walls, but these hiding-places were too obvious for a devious man like Creswell. Tex's gaze ended with him looking at the window behind the desk. He raised himself to orient his position.

Beneath the window was a flat roof and then the road below. Opposite the window was the law office.

He stared at the office until, in a shocked moment, he understood Creswell's intent. Elias's tactic of sneaking George Milligan into town to a position of safety hadn't fooled him. Creswell had known who the prisoner was all along.

George was locked away in a cell across the road and Creswell knew that the location of the Lone Star was locked away in his mind. All he had to do to get that information was to wait for George to be released.

From up here, Creswell could look down at the law office and enjoy a triumph that was especially sweet because Elias thought he'd outguessed him.

After Tex had watched the law office for a minute, Creswell's victory became even more likely when the men who had escorted him to the saloon came into view from down the road. Several other men had joined them and, with determined treads, they spread out and took up positions in the alleys on either side of the law office.

Clearly Creswell had stopped playing the waiting game. With the sheriff out of town and with the one man who could foil his plans trapped in his office, he now planned to break George from his cell.

'Damn,' Tex muttered and swept a ledger to the floor.

'I hope your search isn't damaging my property,' Creswell said. He failed to hide the delight in his voice. 'If it is, I'll make you put everything back in its rightful place.'

Confirmation that Creswell had planned his move well came when the men outside the sheriff's office started gesturing at each other to co-ordinate their assault. He also heard a murmured conversation in the corridor, which confirmed that Mitch was still there.

Tex considered the door. He dismissed bursting

through and taking them on as being too risky. So instead, he picked up a chair and turned to the window.

'I'm coming out now, Creswell,' he called. 'And then I'm leaving town with the Lone Star.'

He didn't wait for a response. With a roll of the shoulders, he hurled the chair at the window, catching it in the middle of Creswell's name and generating a satisfying explosion of glass. Then he followed the chair.

When he landed on the short roof, he lay down and surveyed the scene below. The men who had been moving in on the law office were scurrying into hiding to either side of the door, Tex's sudden action having worried them into taking evasive action.

Since he was lying down and presenting a difficult target, nobody took a shot at him. So he reckoned he could hole up here for a while in a position that commanded an excellent view of the scene.

The main danger could come from the window above, so he crawled along the roof to lie to the side of the window, where he awaited developments. He didn't have to wait for long.

Creswell appeared in the saloon doorway down below and urged his men to act quickly before he scurried out of view down the boardwalk. His men tried a variety of covered places as they searched for a position where they could get a clear shot at Tex.

Tex held his fire until they presented easier

targets, but their positions didn't provide cover from all directions, so Deputy Haywood edged open the door of the law office to blast lead at them. A returned volley kicked splinters from the doorframe and made him slam the door shut hastily.

The gunfire encouraged more men to join the battle from various parts of town, and they all aimed their guns at the law office.

Tex felt the folded diary pages in his pocket, which he hadn't had the time to read yet. He hoped that the truth was written down there, in case Creswell won through.

Scraping and then a thud sounded in the office above as someone, presumably Mitch, forced their way in.

While keeping half an eye on the window, Tex was picking out which potential target he thought would make a decisive move first when a slug sliced into the roof a foot to his side. Nobody should have been able to get that close to him from down below and, with a wince, he realized it hadn't come from the road.

He ran his gaze across the upper floors of the buildings opposite. His perusal ended with him looking at an open window in the hotel three buildings along from the law office.

He couldn't see anyone in the room beyond, but a moment later a rifle slipped into view and was rested on the sill. Then behind it a man's hat rose into view.

Tex waited until he had a clear shot, but then,

from the corner of his eye, he saw movement. He flicked his gaze to the side to see Mitch vaulting out of the window as, in a co-ordinated move, the man in the hotel jumped up.

Tex rolled to the right, to lie on his back, the action saving him from a slug that tore into the roof beside his leg. On his back, he aimed up at Mitch, who was teetering on the roof as he struggled to keep his balance after his hurried leap.

Tex made him pay for his lack of agility and hammered lead up into his chest. The blow made Mitch drop his gun, his eyes wide with surprise that Tex had bested him. He fell forward on to his knees and then went all his length to lie sprawled over Tex's legs, pinning him down.

This movement didn't concern Tex, as a second rifle shot then tore out and punched into Mitch's still body, saving Tex from injury.

Using the body as cover, Tex took careful aim across the road. Before the shooter could fire again, he cannoned a deadly shot into the man's chest, which stood him upright in the window before he tumbled forward and fell to the ground below.

With hurried gestures Tex rolled Mitch's dead weight off him. In a tangle of limp arms and legs, Mitch disappeared from view over the edge of the roof, but his departure was followed by the arrival of a second man, who jumped down from the window.

This man landed more adroitly than Mitch had

done and, with his feet planted wide apart, he swung his gun round to aim down at Tex.

In desperation Tex kicked out. His boot caught the man's ankle and sent him to one knee.

The action veered the man's aim and made him send his shot winging over Tex's head. But with Tex lying in a vulnerable position, his assailant reacted quickly and continued his motion to drop down heavily on Tex's chest before Tex could fire.

Then they struggled. Both men kept hold of their own guns while trying to push the other man away with their free hands.

Neither man was effective; they rolled to the wall and then away. Then, with a lurch, a giddy sense of weightlessness overcame Tex as they rolled over the side.

He and his assailant plummeted through the air. Brief cries of alarm slipped from both men's lips.

Then they slammed down on to the hardpan.

Tex hadn't had enough time to work out how to cushion his fall, but it was possible that his rigidity saved him from serious injury.

Despite coming off relatively unscathed, all the air blasted from his chest and he lay stunned. The other man moaned before he rolled away to lie still and unconscious.

Tex reckoned he was close to losing consciousness himself, so he forced himself to get to his knees and crawl towards the saloon. He swayed and was about to tip over, but his waving hand slapped against a post on the boardwalk. He used the post to still his motion. Then he dragged himself upright.

His vision was still unfocused, so he concentrated on self-preservation. He pushed off and moved towards where he reckoned the saloon door would be.

While snaking across the boardwalk, he heard Creswell shouting, but his orders sounded as if they were being made far away and he couldn't make out the words. He shook his head and managed to form two separate and swirling visions of the saloon wall.

He couldn't make those two images form into one, so, with a hand held out ready to swing himself inside, he walked towards the door that was swimming in and out of focus to his left. The hand slapped against something cold and he had a disorienting vision of a ghostly form looking at him.

'Shoot him,' someone shouted, the words coming from close by.

As gunfire tore out, Tex put his head down and pushed on. The cold object shattered, destroying the ghostly image and, in a moment of clarity, Tex realized he'd been looking at his own reflection in the saloon window.

Then he tumbled forward and fell through the broken window. Another volley rang out, but the shots clattered into the saloon wall as he pitched down on to a table, then rolled to the side to lie on the floor.

He glanced around the empty saloon room and heard groaning coming from near by. For a moment he thought he'd landed on someone again. But he was wrong.

He was the one who was groaning.

CHAPTER 10

'You couldn't have found proof that I killed Oliver Lee,' Rafferty said after he'd handed over his six-shooter. 'I'm innocent, as is Bud.'

'I hate the way you can say that with conviction,' Sheriff Bryce said. He swung his horse round to stand alongside him. 'Save your excuses for your trial when you'll get a better chance to explain yourself than you gave Oliver and the others you killed.'

'Nobody else has died that I know of.' Rafferty winced. 'Are you saying Oliver wasn't the only one?'

'After I arrested Bud I followed the trail of bodies. My guide was your debt book.' Bryce drew the book from his pocket and waved it at him. 'All the people you've collected debts from over the last two days are now dead.'

'I'd have had nothing to gain by doing that,' Rafferty murmured, still incredulous that Creswell would go to such lengths to teach him a lesson for defying him.

Bryce pointed towards town. 'You can either ride into town ahead of me, or face down over the back of your horse.'

Rafferty considered Bryce's stern gaze. Then, with a nod, he moved his horse on to ride ahead of him.

They rode at a steady pace and in silence. Every mile they covered only helped to increase Rafferty's feeling of resignation.

He had just caught his first sight of town when anger defeated his numb feeling. He stopped on the crest of a rise where he could look down on the settlement.

He waited until the lawman had drawn alongside and was casting him a harsh glare that ordered him to move on before he returned a pleasant and, he hoped, honest smile.

'You're wrong about me,' he said. 'I hate Creswell Washington more even than you do.'

Bryce shrugged, appearing as if, despite his comments back at Devil's Canyon, he might be prepared to listen.

'I'd like to believe you. Give me Creswell and I'll speak up for you.'

'I've been taking him on in my own way.' Rafferty considered Bryce's sceptical expression and took a deep breath. 'I stole money from his safe and gave it to the people who owed him. Creswell found out and he killed them to teach me a lesson.'

Bryce tipped back his hat while shaking his head.

'Nobody would make up a story like that one, so I'm inclined to believe you, but that defence doesn't make me feel any different about you.'

'It should. I was once your deputy, except I made a mistake. I've been paying for it ever since.'

'Quit with the excuses. You tarnished everything the badge stood for when you sided with Creswell. What makes it worse is that you've always been able to turn things round, and yet you haven't. Now others have paid the worst price of all, not you.'

Rafferty lowered his head. 'You're right. No matter what the consequences, I should have acted earlier.'

Bryce started to shake his head, but Rafferty's gruff tone must have convinced him that he could trust him because he stopped and considered him. He moved his horse closer and lowered his own tone to a more conciliatory level.

'Are you saying Creswell has a hold over you that you can't break?'

Rafferty breathed a sigh of relief, now finding that he was eager to unburden himself.

'He has. On the night Loudon Sutherland died and the Lone Star went missing, Creswell saw what he wanted to see, but it was enough to force me to resign. Then bit by bit he drew me in.' Rafferty waited until Bryce raised his eyebrows, silently asking the obvious question. 'I don't know where the Lone Star is, but sometimes I reckon I saw enough to work it out.'

For long moments Bryce considered. When he spoke, his low tone suggested his offer was genuine.

'If you help me to destroy Creswell, I'll believe you.'

'Then I will.' Rafferty breathed a sigh of relief. 'And I'm glad I've finally got an ally whom I can confide in.'

Bryce snorted a laugh. 'I wouldn't go that far. This—'

Distant gunfire sounded, echoing between the buildings in the town ahead, closely followed by several rapid volleys.

The two men looked at each other and winced. Then Rafferty joined Bryce in galloping off.

They rode on for only a minute before they got their second surprise. A line of riders appeared from around a sprawling line of boulders ahead.

These men were moving on to town at speed and they were coming from the area to the north of Devil's Canyon. Although Rafferty was too far away to discern their faces, he could make a good guess about who they were and what they were doing.

There were six men and they were looking ahead at the town where gunfire was blasting out sporadically. As the riders had no more than a 200-yard lead on them, they would arrive only a short while before they did.

When they were fifty yards behind the trailing rider, Rafferty and Bryce slowed to match their speed. They were approaching the edge of town when that man looked back.

He registered their presence with a flinch, then relayed the news to the other men. When they looked back, it was Rafferty's turn to flinch.

'I recognize those men,' Rafferty shouted. He concentrated on riding for a few seconds before he continued. 'I only went to Diamond Springs once, two years ago, but I saw some of the townsfolk. It seems they've returned to take on Creswell.'

Bryce grunted confirmation that he'd had the same thought. He said nothing else until they'd closed on the riders. Then he hailed them.

With an exchange of glances amongst themselves, the men agreed to slow and let Bryce draw alongside. They were now a hundred yards from the start of the main drag into town and as there'd been no gunfire for the last two minutes, Bryce slowed to speak to them.

'You Diamond Springs men planning to give me trouble?' he asked.

'Nope,' Elias Sutherland said. 'We aim to help you.'

'I'm pleased to hear that and I'm pleased to see you've turned up alive, but I plan to restore the peace. That means stopping this situation getting out of control and turning Bear Creek into the kind of town Diamond Springs became.'

'We agree.' Elias raised a hand in a sign of acquiescing. 'We'll follow your orders, unless one of us gets to Creswell Washington before you do. Then you won't be able to stop us shooting him up.'

Bryce considered this offer with a rueful smile before he beckoned them to draw back and let him take the lead.

Rafferty moved on into the bunch and nodded to the men he recognized. These men returned vague salutes that showed they recognized him, although they were still struggling to place him.

At a fast trot they entered town, where Rafferty saw that most of the townsfolk had scurried into safety and that the gunfight was centred around the law office. At least a dozen men were laying siege to the building.

Rafferty could see Creswell's intent, although he was surprised that he had acted so openly. The fact that he had meant he must be close to getting his hands on the Lone Star, or else it wouldn't be worth his taking the risk that he might not be able to avoid the consequences.

Bryce slowed to a halt in the middle of the road and the rest of the men spread out around him.

'Creswell Washington!' he shouted. 'You have one chance to save yourself.'

Some of the men who were out on the road looked up, then ducked down again behind cover, but Creswell didn't show.

Long moments passed until the door to the law office opened and Deputy Haywood acknowledged them with a relieved wave, but then one of the gunmen took a shot at him. The lead sliced into the door as Haywood dived for cover.

That reaction proved too much for Bryce and, with quick gestures, he ordered his group to take cover on either side of the road. He beckoned Rafferty and Elias to stay with him, so the three men dismounted and hurried into hiding behind a row of barrels that stood outside the mercantile.

Here they had a good view down the road to the law office.

'What's your orders, Sheriff?' Elias asked, but Bryce said nothing as he cast a long look at Rafferty.

'I didn't know Creswell was planning this,' Rafferty said, spreading his hands, 'so I can't tell you what his next move will be.'

For long moments Bryce considered him, then he gave a brief nod. He handed back Rafferty's weapon.

'The important thing is to find out where he's gone to ground.'

'If what I remember about him still holds true,' Elias said, 'his men will capture George Milligan while he keeps himself safe.'

'I agree,' Rafferty said. 'That'll give him a chance of talking his way out of this if we foil the raid.'

'Not this time,' Bryce said. He raised his head to consider the scene. 'I'll go after Creswell and end this siege before it gets out of hand. You people keep his men pinned down.'

He patted both men on the back. Then, bent double, he hurried to the side of the mercantile and away. Elias and Rafferty shuffled closer to each other and, with the barrels as cover, they awaited developments.

'I remember you,' Elias said after five minutes had passed with nobody making a move to break the impasse.

Rafferty nodded. 'You were keeping watch at the Lone Star saloon's window.'

The two men looked at each other; Rafferty could tell that Elias was minded to speak of the many incidents that had taken place in Diamond Springs two years ago.

'Have you seen any more men from Diamond Springs recently?' he asked instead.

'No, but then again, I wasn't looking out for any.'

A gunshot ripped out, the first of a volley of lead from Creswell's men that tore into the Dark Night saloon. Returning gunfire came from the doorway and as neither Bryce nor Elias's men had gone that way, Rafferty was pleased to see that they had at least one other ally.

'There were three men,' Elias said as he also looked at the saloon with his brow furrowed. 'They were heading to Diamond Springs, but I'd heard they got shot up.'

Rafferty nodded. 'Would one of them be Horatio Wilde?'

'Yeah.'

'I hadn't realized those men were originally from Diamond Springs.' Rafferty frowned and lowered his tone to a sympathetic one. 'But you heard right. They're dead.'

Elias muttered under his breath, then turned to him, presumably to ask for more details, but another volley tore out at the saloon.

This time Rafferty saw that Creswell's men were aiming at the man who had appeared briefly at the window: Tex Callahan.

Rafferty smiled, noting that Tex had been as good as his word in opposing Creswell.

'At least Tex has got himself into a position to help us,' Elias said, pointing. 'He'll more than make up for the loss of Horatio and the others.'

'I didn't know you knew Tex too. But don't trust him. Tex is his own man.' Rafferty's voice had become gruff, making Elias look at him. 'He killed Horatio.'

CHAPTER 11

Lying on his belly in the doorway, Tex fired at Creswell's men, splaying his gunfire around as he kept them down.

Elias and his brother Brewster took advantage of the lull and worked their way along to the building beside the saloon before taking cover out of his sight.

Tex reckoned he had also seen Rafferty Horn amongst the defenders. He had run down the road to join the men who were in hiding outside the bank and had encouraged them to cover Elias and Brewster.

Rapid footfalls pounded down the boardwalk, heralding Elias's arrival. Elias swung through the door, then doubled back, leant outside and beckoned Brewster, who needed Elias's and Tex's covering fire before he arrived at a scrambling hurry.

'Are the rest coming?' Tex asked.

'No,' Elias said, his voice deep and odd-sounding.

'They're staying where they are.'

'Then that means we're in decent positions to stop Creswell. But we'll have to be careful. Creswell's sneaky and he'll have a plan in mind.'

'From what I gather he's not the only one who's sneaky.'

Tex glanced at Elias, who was glaring at him with his eyes narrowed. Tex conceded his point with a nod.

'Not sneaky enough sometimes.' He rubbed his ribs ruefully acknowledging the bruises that his fall from the roof had given him. 'What's the lawman's plan?'

'Sheriff Bryce aims to find Creswell and then to end this siege quickly.'

As with most of Elias's comments, his tone had been irritated. Tex couldn't blame him as he had clearly put time and effort into his plan, yet he had made the mistake of not taking full account of Creswell's ruthless nature.

Tex beckoned Elias to take the left-hand window while Brewster took the right. Brewster moved into position at a scamper. He instantly picked out a target and fired.

Tex nodded approvingly, but Elias didn't move to the other window. Tex waved, ordering him to move, but instead, Elias stomped his feet as he took up a position behind him where he would be able to see over the swing doors.

'You can be seen standing there,' Tex said. 'Move.'

'Not doing that, Tex.'

Elias's tone had become sombre. This time Tex reckoned he knew what had annoyed him. It had been inevitable that someone would eventually find out that he'd killed Horatio Wilde, but he had hoped this wouldn't happen until after he'd earned the Diamond Springs folk's respect.

'Not going to lie to you.' Tex settled his posture on the floor. He kept looking straight ahead at the boardwalk opposite where Creswell's men were still staying down. 'I didn't know who Horatio was.'

'Finish your excuses. Then I'll kill you.'

'I have none. I shot up Horatio and the others. I didn't give them a chance to explain themselves. Then again, I wasn't to know they only wanted to tell me about your plans. If you hadn't been so secretive, I wouldn't have ended up killing them.'

From the corner of his eye, Tex saw Brewster glance at Elias, his narrowed eyes acknowledging that Tex had made a valid point. Elias exhaled his breath and Tex caught a brief flicker as his shadow moved on the floor.

'Keep looking forward,' Elias said. 'And keep looking outside, Brewster.'

Tex reckoned Elias was now distracted, so he straightened his back, giving the impression he was straining his neck to look at something outside.

The shadow flickered again, presumably as Elias

followed his gaze, so Tex turned his motion into a roll to the side while swinging his gun back over his head, held two-handed. But when he landed on his back he stayed his hand.

Elias hadn't been distracted. He still had his gun aimed down at him.

'Don't,' Tex said with a shake of the head. 'I'm your only chance of defeating Creswell Washington.'

'You are,' Elias said, his tone resigned, 'and that's what makes this so hard.'

He frowned and, for a relieved moment, Tex thought he'd move on to the window without firing. Then an explosion of light burst from Elias's gun. Pain exploded in Tex's lower chest as if a great weight had been dropped on him.

Unable to control his movements, Tex curled into a ball. His gun dropped from his slack fingers with a clatter.

Through pained eyes he looked up for as far as he was able, to find that both Elias and Brewster were now standing over him.

'Mistake,' Tex muttered, his breath coming in short gasps that rustled the dust on the floor. 'Made . . . big . . . mistake.'

'Maybe I did.' Elias knelt and ran his fingers across the floor. He raised them to look at the copious blood that dribbled down the back of his hand and then dripped to the floor. 'But did you make a mistake? Did you leave Horatio to die in a pool of his own blood?'

'Didn't know.' Talking was now so hard that Tex wasn't sure if he'd spoken aloud. 'You didn't tell me nothing.'

'Maybe before your life blood dribbles out on to the floor you might regret your mistake.'

Elias stood, which took him out of Tex's sight. As Tex was sure he couldn't straighten his body so that he could watch Elias when he finished him off, he fixed his gaze on the floor.

Long moments passed in which Tex expected that every tortured breath would be his last. But instead, Elias's boots clumped on.

Then the doors creaked as he and Brewster slipped outside. Rapid footfalls sounded as they ran down the boardwalk, their progress attracting several gunshots.

'You made the mistake,' Tex grunted to himself. 'You left me alive.'

Tex tried to let the thought of revenge give him the strength to move, but it didn't work; he just lay where he'd fallen, feeling tired as the damp patch beneath him spread.

Strangely, the only matter that troubled him was that now he'd never find out the truth about the Lone Star. Then the thought came that perhaps there was still time.

He reached for his pocket and, after two failed attempts, he slipped his hand inside. Then, moving carefully, he removed the folded sheets of paper that

George Milligan had wanted him to have.

These sheets were the final pages of his account of the incident in Diamond Springs. Elias had claimed that only later, when George had read his own words, had he worked out the truth about the diamond.

Tex moved the papers round to place them before his eyes. Then, using the floor for leverage, he prised them open.

The first sheet was blank, as was the second, and as were the other two. There was no answer written there, after all.

Tex allowed himself a brief smile. He closed the papers. Then he closed his eyes.

With the gunfire from the Dark Night Saloon having stopped, Creswell's assault on the law office began in earnest.

His men laid down a burst of gunfire that shattered both windows. With Deputy Haywood pinned down inside, two men ran for the door where they stood on either side.

One man risked standing in front of the door to kick it open, after which he beat a hasty retreat. Then the two men stood against the wall, picking the right time to burst in.

This was the moment when Elias and his men showed their hand. Although Rafferty still hoped that Sheriff Bryce would be able to stop this siege before blood was shed, he joined them.

His first shot was at the man standing to the left of the door. The slug clattered feet wide, but he was pleased he'd now taken his first positive action against Creswell.

He took more careful aim and hammered a deadly shot into the man's chest that made him drop to the boardwalk. That sight encouraged the other man to risk moving into the law office. He went in low and a rapid exchange of fire sounded.

Rafferty caught the nearest man's eye and he returned a shrug, but they got their answer soon enough when someone shouted triumphantly inside the law office. Then several men hurried over to the door.

Elias's men tried to subdue the attackers with a rapid volley of gunshots, but their shots flew wide while in return the running attackers picked out their targets with impressive accuracy.

Two of Elias's men went down, clutching their arms, while Brewster got a shot to the chest. After that, the remaining men stayed down. Rafferty stilled his own fire to appraise the situation; he couldn't find any grounds for optimism.

Tex was no longer helping with the defence of the law office, so Elias's group was the only opposition to Creswell and they were heavily outnumbered, outgunned, and outclassed in gun skills even before they'd taken casualties.

Unless Bryce could find Creswell, they wouldn't be

able to stop these men from taking George from the jail. After that, if what Elias had told him before he'd gone to the saloon proved accurate, he would be given no choice other than to lead Creswell to the Lone Star.

That thought reminded Rafferty that Bryce had said there was only one way to stop this gunfight, and Rafferty had one advantage over the sheriff: he knew how Creswell thought.

He gestured at the nearest man to get his attention. Unfortunately, that man was too busy casting worried glances at his wounded colleagues. Rafferty backed away to the wall, then slipped out of the view of the gunslingers to head down an alley beside the bank.

He reached the back of the bank and worked his way down the backs of the buildings until he reached the Dark Night saloon. There was no door available, but he found a window. He wasted no time in smashing it, scraping away the shards of glass, and clambering inside.

He found himself in a storeroom where all was silent. In the enclosed space, even the chaos out on the road sounded far away.

Quickly, he made his way to the main saloon room, finding it abandoned. He hurried towards the stairs, but then he slid to a halt halfway across the room. His first glance around had failed to spot the body lying in front of the doorway, and when he moved to a position that let him see the face, he recognized Tex Callahan.

Despite the urgent need to act, he approached him, and found that he was breathing shallowly, although Tex didn't register his presence. Elias and Brewster had left the saloon quickly and it was clear what had happened here.

'After what happened in Diamond Springs,' he said, 'I never thought I'd see you bested.'

The comment made Tex stir and murmur a moan, but as Rafferty didn't have the skills to help him, he hurried to the stairs and then went up them. He'd reached the corridor at the top when a muffled explosion sounded some distance away.

He reckoned the noise had been that of George's cell being broken into, so, while the reverberations were still echoing, he hurried to the door to Creswell's office and went inside.

Creswell was at the window in the shadows, as Rafferty had expected, looking down through the broken glass at the scene below.

'I knew you'd be the first one to find me,' Creswell said without turning. 'Sheriff Bryce is scurrying around town, but he hasn't considered the most obvious place to look.'

'It's only obvious to someone who knows you,' Rafferty said. He walked forward slowly and confirmed that nobody else was in the room.

'Then we really do understand each other.'

Creswell beckoned Rafferty to come to the window. 'Join me and share in my triumph.'

Creswell would know that he'd drawn a gun and that he could shoot him in the back.

The fact that Creswell was unperturbed meant he'd taken steps to ensure that if Rafferty fired, the information Cresswell had about him would become common knowledge. That no longer mattered as much as regaining his independence and integrity, but still he holstered his gun before he crossed the room to stand at Creswell's side.

Outside, Creswell's men were taking up defensive positions before they brought George out of the law office. They'd formed a phalanx that guarded all aspects while an open wagon approached. Elias and his men were all staying down.

'I can't claim to fully understand you,' Rafferty said. 'I never expected you to make such a committed move as this one.'

'It's not my usual style, but this time the prize is worth it.'

'It'd better be. I saw Mitch Sawyer lying dead out there.'

A momentary tightening of the skin around the eyes was Creswell's only reaction.

'Mitch didn't die in vain. He helped to put an end to my main threat.'

'You're wrong. Your main problem is still to come. You'll never talk your way out of shooting up a law office and kidnapping a prisoner.' Rafferty paused before he finished his list. 'And shooting up everyone who owed you money.'

This last item made Creswell smile. 'I don't intend to try. I have plans elsewhere, but never let it be said that I leave loose ends behind. No debtors, no enemies, no Tex Callahan.'

'Aren't I a loose end?'

Creswell snorted a single laugh. 'I'm sorry to tell you this, Rafferty, but you're not important enough for your continued existence to worry me.'

'A man with a gun should always be considered important.'

Creswell glanced at Rafferty's holster with an unconcerned air before returning to watching the scene outside, where George Milligan was now being led through the door. Any chance that Elias had enough firepower to stop his being taken away receded when Creswell's men got him to the wagon without mishap.

'Respect is only granted to those with the motivation to fire,' Creswell said, 'and you haven't got that.'

'You've provided me with enough today. You had Oliver Lee and your other debtors killed for nothing. That means I no longer care about my own fate.'

'I know,' Creswell said in a weary tone, as if the power he had over Rafferty no longer gave him pleasure now that he was about to get something he wanted even more. 'But your statement proves you do still care about what happens to others.'

Creswell pointed down into the road where Bud was now being led outside. He was moving in his usual lumbering, docile manner as he joined George in the back of the wagon.

'Bud has always done your bidding,' Rafferty said, 'without question. You won't harm him.'

'I won't, but there's no end to the harm he can inflict on others, especially those who won't answer my questions.'

'Don't make him hurt George.'

'I hope I won't have to. But it's interesting that you care about Bud. Keeping him from going too far again has always been the real hold I have over you.' Creswell turned to him and raised an eyebrow. 'Isn't it?'

Rafferty gulped then gave a brief nod, acknowledging Creswell's astuteness.

'It is.'

'So you can rest assured I won't make Bud do anything to George other than threaten him. But if you try to stop me, I'll make him do his worst.'

Rafferty could do nothing but lower his head. Worse, he knew that even though he'd never get a better chance to kill Creswell, he wouldn't draw his gun.

CHAPTER 12

'You got here too late,' Rafferty said. 'Creswell's gone.'

Sheriff Bryce still glanced around the office before he came over to join Rafferty at the window.

'Did you see him leave?'

'Yeah.' Rafferty pointed to the edge of town and the receding cloud of dust the wagon and riders had made as they'd left for Diamond Springs.

'And yet you didn't try to stop him?'

Rafferty shook his head, breaking himself free of the torpor that had consumed him since, with such casual contempt, Creswell had dismissed him as a threat.

'I couldn't,' he said, his voice low.

'I thought so,' Bryce spat with almost as much contempt as Creswell had shown. 'I should never have listened to your promises.'

'And I should never have made them,' Rafferty

murmured. He turned with his hands spread in a show of surrender.

Bryce did as Rafferty expected. He disarmed him and then walked him down to the saloon room.

Tex's body was no longer lying in front of the door, although the large bloodstain he'd left suggested it hadn't turned out well for him. Rafferty was pleased to see that Elias's men had fared better.

Several men had been wounded, but they were all alive and the fit ones were awaiting Bryce's instructions. The sheriff informed them that as soon as he'd thrown Rafferty into a cell they'd follow Creswell.

Rafferty's new status as a prisoner made Elias cast him an odd look, but Bryce didn't explain his decision as he took Rafferty across the road.

When they arrived at the law office, Doctor Tomlinson was kneeling beside the supine body of Deputy Haywood. He met Bryce's gaze and shook his head before covering Haywood with a blanket.

With a muttered oath, Bryce pushed Rafferty towards the only intact cell with so much force that he stumbled. Rafferty righted himself and turned to face Bryce's red face and bunched fists, the sheriff's anger showing he deemed Rafferty partly responsible for the deputy's death.

'At least,' Tomlinson said, speaking calmly, 'he should be the only one to die.'

'At least that,' Bryce spat. His hollow tone didn't sound placated.

'Does that mean,' Rafferty said, 'that Tex Callahan will be fine?'

'If that's who the man in the saloon was,' Tomlinson said, 'then he will be once I've worked on him.'

Tomlinson nodded to Bryce, then turned to the door. Bryce didn't speak again until he'd left.

'If this Tex is a friend of yours, I won't lose sleep over his fate.'

'You should,' Rafferty said. 'He hates Creswell.'

Bryce pointed at the cell and, without further comment, Rafferty walked inside. He sat down and tucked his legs up on the cot as he watched Bryce get ready to leave.

Elias arrived to report that when Bryce was ready to go only himself and two of his men would be able to accompany him. The other two men, along with Brewster, were too incapacitated.

His brother had suffered a glancing cut across the ribs, along with a sprained right wrist when he'd fallen. Despite that, as Brewster was the fittest of the wounded, the sheriff left him in charge of the office.

Bryce didn't speak to Rafferty again, neither did he even look his way as he hurried outside.

Through the broken windows, Rafferty watched him gather the fit men from Diamond Springs together and deliver instructions. Then, at a gallop, the four riders left town in a straggling line to pursue Creswell.

Rafferty didn't expect to see any of them alive again.

'You need to rest,' Doctor Tomlinson said, placing a hand down on Tex's chest.

Tex shoved the hand away, took a deep breath, then tried to swing himself up to a sitting position on the table. This proved to be an unwise manoeuvre as he was even weaker than he'd thought he was, so his efforts only succeeded in rolling him on to his side.

'What have you done to me?' Tex murmured.

'I stitched you up,' Tomlinson said, 'and if you don't rest, I'll have to stitch you up again.'

'I can't rest. I have to go.'

'So you want to go in search of the man who shot you, do you?' Tex didn't answer, but Tomlinson still sighed while looking to the ceiling. 'Well, you can, but not yet. The bullet shattered a rib.'

'Is the bullet out?'

'It went in and out of its own accord, but the wound needs time to settle or you'll get an infection. And after all the blood you lost, you're too weak to do anything but fall over.'

Tex snorted a laugh to confirm he wouldn't be taking that advice and held out a hand for the doctor to help him off the table. Tomlinson glared at him, but with a shake of the head he helped him sit.

When he was on his feet, Tex pushed the doctor's hands away. Then he stood swaying while Tomlinson held out his hands waiting for him to fall.

When his patient stayed upright, Tomlinson stood back and gestured to the door with an indulgent look that said that in a few minutes he'd be telling Tex that he'd been right to advise that he wouldn't get far.

That look made Tex determined to prove him wrong and, with faltering steps, he embarked on the journey to the door and then outside.

He broke the trip down into short passages, where he aimed for furniture, sections of the wall and the door; this helped him to reach the boardwalk where he propped himself up against the surgery wall.

Time had passed since the gunfight and it was now dark. The coolness helped to revive his senses and make him feel that he hadn't been foolish to leave so soon after waking, after all.

After a few minutes Tomlinson poked his head out through the door and looked down at the boardwalk. He registered surprise with raised eyebrows on seeing that Tex wasn't lying there. He looked up to meet his gaze.

'I'm fine,' Tex croaked.

Tomlinson waved a dismissive hand at him and then, while shaking his head, he left him to his own devices.

Once he'd been left alone Tex accepted, despite his bravado, that he wasn't fit enough to sit a horse. Even crossing the road he felt was beyond him.

Revenge being impossible for the moment, he turned his attention to seeking out the nearest hotel.

Using the same technique that had got him outside the doctor's house, he went on short journeys, picking distances that he was sure he could cover. After several brief journeys, the refreshing night air made him think he could now cover longer distances, but he kept within his limits.

The Dark Night saloon was on the other side of the road. The establishment was closed, suggesting that while he'd been unconscious events had moved on, but he didn't mind waiting to find out what had happened.

That resolve changed when he reached the law office.

The windows were broken, the door had been torn away, and bullet holes peppered the walls. Despite the recent chaos, a light was on inside.

When he looked in through a window he saw Brewster, the man who had been with Elias when he'd shot him, sitting at a desk.

The sight made him swing away from the window and press his back to the wall while taking deep breaths. This man hadn't been responsible for his current state, but he hadn't tried to stop Elias from shooting him either.

He took stock of his physical condition again and decided that he was fit enough to get inside quickly and kill Brewster, but getting away afterwards would be beyond his capabilities for now.

So he pushed himself away from the wall and embarked on the trip to the hitching rail, where he worked his way along. When he'd passed the door, he again looked in at Brewster through the second window, to check that he hadn't been seen.

Brewster was looking elsewhere, and Tex dismissed him from his thoughts as he could now see the row of cells at the back of the office.

One door was swinging open while the door to the second cell was no longer there. In the third cell a solitary man was pacing back and forth: Rafferty Horn, the man who must have told Elias about his mistake in Diamond Springs.

Tex stood upright, the blood pounding in his ears. With a hand clutched to his belly, he took deep breaths to build his strength, then made for the door.

His anger sustained him for long enough to let him keep going without having to make a stop at the door, but by the time he'd reached Brewster's desk his legs were shaking.

He accepted that he must look as ill as he felt, as Brewster, when he looked up, merely considered him with his mouth open. Then he got over his surprise and got up from behind his desk while favouring his side and right arm.

'You're alive,' Bewster murmured.

'No thanks to you,' Tex grunted.

He swung up a fist backhanded, aiming to slap

Brewster's face, but the effort unbalanced him, the punch flew a foot wide and he stumbled.

Brewster put a hand on his shoulder, his expression one of concern, and sought to hold him upright, but anger still burned in Tex's mind.

He pushed his weight against Brewster's chest and forced him back for a pace, then for another, until Brewster was standing against the wall.

Only then did Brewster fight back and try to push him away, but with Tex leaning his weight against him, he couldn't move him using only one hand. This time Tex managed to deliver a backhanded punch to his face.

The blow cracked Brewster's head back against the wall and his eyes glazed as Tex's hand dropped away from him. Heartened that he might prevail, Tex gathered his strength, took a backward pace, and then repeated the blow.

The back of Brewster's head again slapped heavily against the wall, after which he collapsed without making a sound to lie at Tex's feet. Tex then gave in to his weakness and placed a hand on the wall to hold himself upright.

He must have stood there for a while as, when he heard Rafferty speaking to him, the man's voice was strident, as if he'd spoken to Tex several times without getting a reply. Even so, in his weak state, Tex couldn't make out the words.

Not that he was interested in anything that

Rafferty had to say.

He turned, worked his way around the desk, then made his way across the office, to stand before the cells. Only one was intact.

Rafferty was standing on the other side of the door with his hands raised to the bars, watching him with the same expression of concern that Brewster had shown.

'You need to rest,' Rafferty said.

'Sure will,' Tex said, settling his stance. 'And I'll rest easier knowing you didn't get to enjoy double-crossing me after I saved your life.'

Rafferty raised his hands from the bars and stood back.

'You sure are right about that. I've lost in all ways. So get this over with quickly.'

'Don't you want to plead for your life first?'

'No. I ruined my one chance to fight back. Creswell defeated me. He'll get away with the Lone Star now.' Rafferty shrugged. 'And worst of all, the people I tried to help will die and there's nothing anyone can do to save them.'

Tex had come in to the law office resolved to kill Rafferty, but the man's last comment reminded Tex of his earlier decision: that this wasn't a good time for him to seek revenge. He fetched a chair and sat down facing the cell.

'What's happened here since you had me shot?' he asked.

In a monotone Rafferty described the events of earlier that day. When he'd finished, Tex had to agree with his assessment that Creswell now had the best chance he'd ever had of uncovering the truth about the Lone Star.

Thoughtfully, he withdrew the sheets of paper from his pocket and held them up to the light, but they were definitely blank.

'What are they?' Rafferty asked. When Tex explained, he looked aloft, as if he were casting his mind back. 'I never spoke to the bartender, but I know that Loudon Sutherland had a plan to make sure the Lone Star didn't remain lost for ever. George could have worked out what that plan was.'

Tex slapped the pages to the floor in irritation.

'If he did, he didn't write it down, or at least not on these pages.'

'George could have been telling you that the answer was to be found elsewhere in the diary.' Rafferty paced back and forth while tapping his chin. 'Or maybe he could have been trying to fool Creswell by making him believe that the answer was written down on those pages.'

Tex stood up and angrily kicked the papers aside.

'You can spout theories all night, but it won't change one fact. Neither of us knows the answer and only I will be alive to figure it out.'

With anger again clouding his mind, Tex drew his gun and hefted it in his hand.

In his line of work he'd been called upon to kill before, but he'd never killed purely out of anger. Despite what Rafferty had done, as time had passed since he'd been shot, he found that a cold-blooded killing didn't sit easily with him.

He met Rafferty's eye, noting his resigned demeanour that said his failure had browbeaten him and he would welcome an end to his suffering.

That thought made Tex smile, accepting that sometimes there are worse things than the quick resolution of death, but he decided to last out Rafferty's uncertainty about his fate for a while longer.

He continued to toy with the gun, hoping to see Rafferty become concerned, but instead, Rafferty lowered his head. When he looked up, he smiled and spread his hands.

'I know the answer,' he said using a calm and level tone. 'In a way I've always known it, except until you told me about the diary, which detailed the townsfolk and their activities in Diamond Springs, I didn't know that I knew it.'

Tex turned the gun on Rafferty and raised an eyebrow, waiting for him to plead for clemency in return for explaining his latest theory, but Rafferty said nothing more.

For long moments the two men locked gazes and, as Rafferty looked more content than he'd ever seen him, with a slight inclination of the head, Tex lowered the gun.

He aimed to the right and fired, blasting a slug at the lock.

'I guess that makes as much sense as anything else I've heard,' Tex said as, obligingly, the door swung open. 'Let's get Creswell before he finds the Lone Star.'

CHAPTER 13

Despite his promise of being fit enough to take on Creswell Washington, Tex was in a bad way. He was sweating and moaning as he sat sprawled over the seat.

He'd been too weak to sit a horse, so Rafferty had found an open wagon to get them to Diamond Springs. Tex had refused to lie down in the back, but now that they were five miles out of town, he was struggling to avoid slipping off the seat to the ground.

Rafferty drew the wagon to a halt and a minute passed before Tex registered what he'd done.

'You ready to admit defeat and lie down in the back?' Rafferty asked.

'No,' Tex muttered through clenched teeth. He flashed a wan smile. 'But that's only because I haven't got the strength to get there.'

The two men exchanged a grim smile. Then Tex

raised an arm for Rafferty to help him.

Now that they'd stopped, Tex proved to be stronger than Rafferty had feared and he managed to clamber down to the ground quickly. Then, with Rafferty supporting him, he was able to walk round to the back of the wagon where Rafferty helped him up.

When Tex was lying on his back with his head resting on several discarded and folded sacks, he murmured more hopefully about his condition.

'We'll still stay here for a while to give you a break,' Rafferty said, 'otherwise when we reach Diamond Springs you won't be fit enough to take on Creswell.'

In truth, Rafferty still doubted that Tex would be alive when they reached their destination, but his optimistic assessment encouraged Tex to seek a more comfortable position that favoured his wounded side.

'You take care of getting me there,' he said between sharp intakes of breath as he settled down. 'I'll take care of Creswell.'

Rafferty patted his shoulder, then sat back against the side of the wagon, letting Tex get the full benefit of the cool night wind. He'd yet to explain the revelation he'd had back in Bear Creek, and Tex had not pressed him for it: probably he was too exhausted to do so.

Rafferty was grateful for his patience, as it had given him time to think his theory through and the more he considered, the more he believed that he was right.

'Creswell has always been one step ahead of Elias, you, everyone,' he said after a while, 'but I reckon that for the first time I've anticipated his next move.'

For several seconds Tex stayed looking at the night sky until, with a sigh, he turned his head to consider him.

'Tell me.' He mustered a smile. 'Don't worry. I'm too weak to kill you after you've explained.'

Rafferty returned the smile, pleased that he'd decided to unburden himself and remove the hold he had effectively gained over Tex.

'It all comes down to Bud,' he said. 'He'd have been mentioned in the diary.'

Tex glanced aloft as he thought back.

'The diary didn't always provide names, but it often mentioned a big man who helped with the digging. He always followed orders obediently, did more than everyone else, and he never complained.'

'That sounds like Bud.' Rafferty considered and decided he didn't want to tell Tex the full story of how Loudon Sutherland had been killed. 'Creswell said that he's taking him to Diamond Springs to help him extract the truth from George Milligan, but I reckon that was a bluff.'

'And that sounds like Creswell.' Tex took shallow breaths that gradually built in strength. Then he shuffled into a more upright position, leaning on an elbow. 'Are you saying that in reality it's Bud who knows the answer?'

'I reckon that's what Creswell's figured out. Elias wouldn't have got George locked in a jail cell without having a good reason. I reckon it was the safest way he could get someone into town to deliver a message to Bud and find out exactly what orders Loudon gave him.'

'Except he had some luck when Sheriff Bryce delivered Bud to George.' Tex considered. 'And they were in cells next to each other for long enough to work out a plan.'

Rafferty offered a thin smile. 'Let's hope it's a good one.'

It was late into the night when Rafferty drew up the wagon half a mile out of Diamond Springs. On the way he hadn't seen the men he was pursuing and now the town was nestling quietly in the moonlight.

As Creswell hadn't had much time to get to the truth, he was probably still there, so this was the closest he dared to approach before he took stock of the situation. Rafferty also had another worrying task, which must be completed first; so, after confirming that nobody was waiting for them, he slipped off the wagon and hurried round to the back.

His worst fears hadn't materialized, as Tex was sleeping quietly with a hand clutched over his wounded side. When Rafferty clambered into the back, Tex stirred.

'Can you move?' Rafferty asked.

'When I have to,' Tex said, considering him with a pained yet determined expression. 'But not until then.'

Rafferty nodded, getting his meaning that it was up to him to scout around and work out a plan. He looked towards the town, noting it was still quiet.

'You stay here and keep lookout. I'll be back when I know what's happening.'

Tex closed his eyes without replying, making Rafferty sit back on his haunches and wonder if he should keep Tex out of any plans he might form, but after he'd watched him for a minute, Tex opened an eye.

'I'm fit enough to take on Creswell,' Tex said with a small voice, 'but not much else.'

Rafferty nodded and clambered down off the wagon. He slipped off into the night. Fifty yards away, he stopped to memorize the aspect of a sprawling line of boulders behind the wagon so that he could return readily.

Then he embarked on a circular route that scouted around the town. He made sure to move closer at a steady rate so that he could view the buildings from a variety of angles.

He'd covered a quarter of the way around Diamond Springs before he confirmed that someone was actually here. Horses were beside the derelict stables and more were there than he'd seen leave with Creswell.

Closer to the stables, he saw the open wagon on which they'd transported Bud and George Milligan. It stood abandoned, but when he took up a position resting behind a small mound, he saw the gathered men for the first time.

Several men had formed a circle around a guarded fire. Within the circle, two men were taking it in turns to pummel another man.

This man needed to be held up to stand and every time someone released him, he fell to his knees and lay gathering his breath before the beating continued. Rafferty assumed the man was George Milligan, but when the victim crawled into a stray beam of light, he saw that he was Elias Sutherland.

Worse, Rafferty's improving night vision enabled him to pick out more details around the stables.

Under the eaves and out of the moonlight were the two other Diamond Springs men who had left town with Elias. They were sitting slumped against the wall while struggling to remain upright.

Clearly the attempt to take on Creswell had failed, but there was no sign of Sheriff Bryce and that gave Rafferty hope. He looked around the immediate vicinity, then at each of the visible men and then towards the town, searching for him.

He picked out two men standing on either side of the stables door, appearing as if they were guarding it while they watched Elias be beaten. This assumption was confirmed when Creswell Washington appeared in the doorway to gesture at the men pummelling Elias.

One man delivered a last punch that sent Elias to his knees. Then Elias's barely conscious form was pulled to his feet and dragged to the stables with his feet cutting twin furrows in the dirt.

Creswell stood aside to let him be taken into the stables. Then he followed them.

Rafferty awaited developments, but the men outside disbanded and took up positions around the fire, so he assumed nothing would happen for a while.

He also assumed that George and Bud were within, although what was happening to them, he couldn't tell, neither did he want to risk getting close enough to find out.

Instead, he set off for the opposite end of town. Then he worked his way along the derelict buildings towards the stables using the route he'd taken two years ago.

This worrying recollection reminded him that the Lone Star saloon was the closest he could get to the stables while remaining hidden.

He stopped in the same place where Tex had stood yesterday when he'd killed Horatio. From here, he had a good view down the road. He could also see a man lying down on his chest in the building beside the saloon.

This man was watching the stables. When Rafferty edged forward to see more of his form, he saw that it was the sheriff. Heartened, he gave a low whistle, making Bryce roll over on to his back.

When Bryce's gaze centred on him, Rafferty waved, beckoning him to join him. Then he backed away in case Bryce misidentified him.

A few moments later Bryce slipped around the corner of the saloon and faced him. His eyes were so blazing Rafferty wondered if it would have been better not to be recognized.

CHAPTER 14

'The last thing I need,' Sheriff Bryce muttered, 'is your help.'

'I'm sure it was,' Rafferty said, 'but right now I'm all you have.'

'I still don't want you. You're Creswell's right-hand man and an escaped prisoner.' Bryce edged forward until the moonlight caught the sheen of gunmetal on the six-shooter he held low and aimed at his chest. 'But now you've become my first prisoner of the night.'

'And that's your first mistake,' Rafferty said. 'And if you don't change your mind, it'll soon be your last.'

He waited for a sign that the sheriff would relent, but when Bryce stared at him impassively, he looked aloft, appearing resigned. He turned away and raised his hands and Bryce moved forward. His jacket rustled as Bryce thrust the gun up against his back.

Rafferty reckoned Bryce wouldn't want to risk making a noise by shooting him. But in his annoyed state it wouldn't have mattered to Rafferty if he did, so when Bryce pushed him on, he dug in a heel and swirled round.

His sudden motion caught Bryce by surprise and, with a flailing hand, he slapped Bryce's arm, veering his gun hand away and towards the saloon wall.

Quickly, he followed through. He grabbed Bryce's wrist and swung him bodily against the wall.

Bryce's elbow collided with the wall, making the gun fall from his grip. The wall rattled, the noise loud in the night, making both men freeze and listen.

A few moments later, from the direction of the stables, several men spoke up, then Creswell's clear order, cutting through the night, for someone to find out who had made the noise.

'You fool,' Bryce muttered, pushing Rafferty away.

Rafferty pushed back, making Bryce bunch his fists. Then the two men squared off, all thoughts of impending discovery gone.

Bryce stepped over his fallen gun, while Rafferty backed away for a pace. He moved as if to take a second pace, but then he rocked back and launched a punch at Bryce's face.

Bryce ducked beneath the aimed blow, so, at the last moment, Rafferty converted the motion into one in which he slapped his arm down on Bryce's back.

He locked hands and pressed down on the sheriff's shoulders making Bryce bend double. Then he tried to wrestle him to the ground.

Bryce twisted on the spot and thrust an elbow into Rafferty's stomach that blasted the air from his chest. As the sudden pain made Rafferty loosen his hold and release him, Bryce stood up straight and used the momentum of the motion to deliver a swiping blow to Rafferty's cheek, which sent him reeling into the wall.

This time it was Rafferty's turn to make the wall rattle as he slid down it and ended up sitting on the ground. Bryce collected his gun and stood over him, but before he could act, two sets of footfalls sounded close by, making him swing away to look towards the stables.

What he saw there made Bryce wince and then turn to hurry away around the opposite corner of the saloon. Then, as an afterthought, he turned back and thrust out a hand to Rafferty, who gratefully took it and let Bryce drag him to his feet.

Groggily, he staggered after the sheriff and rounded the corner where both men pressed themselves to the wall in the dark.

Shuffling sounded on the road at the spot where they'd both been standing a few moments earlier and Rafferty could imagine a silent exchange of views going on as their two pursuers sought to find them.

Accordingly, Bryce gave orders to Rafferty silently.

He pointed to the far end of the wall then bent his fingers to signify that Rafferty should go into the Lone Star saloon through the back way.

As Bryce now appeared to have accepted his help, albeit after finding that he had no choice, Rafferty walked off quietly.

Using the knowledge he'd gained when he'd seen the saloon in daylight, he reached the corner without mishap. Then he started planning his journey across the interior, but a noise sounded on the other side of the wall.

A moment later a man appeared, his form shrouded in the gloom.

Rafferty lashed out, catching the man with a glancing blow that spun him round. His opponent grunted, the noise again sounding louder than would be usual in the daytime.

As he now needed to act quickly, Rafferty drew his gun, turned it round, and clubbed the back of the man's head. The man went down with a clatter.

Rafferty then moved on to carry out his order, but from the corner of his eye he saw that Bryce was now struggling to subdue the other man.

The two men writhed while turning on the spot. Gunmetal gleamed in reflected beams of moonlight as they fought to turn their guns on each other.

Rafferty broke into a run, making both men glance his way and, with the distraction breaking their concentration, they wrestled themselves clear of each other. Twin gunshots roared, the explosions of light illuminating the wall and providing Rafferty with a flashed image of both men standing poised and shocked.

Then they both keeled over.

Rafferty reached their sides while they were still settling to the ground. He turned to Bryce's assailant first. He kicked away his gun and dragged him aside into the moonlight.

The man didn't complain and the improved light let Rafferty see that he'd been shot fatally in the neck.

He turned back to Bryce, but the lawman was in a bad way too. Bryce batted Rafferty's hands away weakly, then clutched his chest as he worked his way backwards to rest against the wall.

'I need to get you out of town,' Rafferty said.

'Too late for that,' Bryce murmured, his voice full of pain.

'I've brought a wagon. I'll fetch it.' Rafferty gave a smile that Bryce probably couldn't see. 'One more wounded helper will be fine with me.'

'Who else?'

'Tex Callahan. He's the gunslinger who hates Creswell.'

'Murderers, outlaws, gunslingers . . . that's all you know.' Bryce grunted. 'Get out of my sight while you still can.'

'You've got me wrong,' Rafferty snapped, now

angry. 'You've always got me wrong. Perhaps if you hadn't sent me here two years ago, none of this would have happened.'

He waited for a reply, but Bryce wouldn't look at him, although his firm jaw said that his comment had registered. Rafferty entertained the hope that Bryce would accept that their enmity was down to his guilt about avoiding a difficult situation two years ago, but Creswell's men were approaching.

This time they'd come in force and they were shouting instructions to each other as they planned their assault.

Rafferty put a hand on Bryce's shoulder, but the sheriff shrugged him off.

'I'll deal with Creswell the right way,' Bryce murmured, his voice faint, 'and that's without you.'

The footfalls were now sounding only yards away from the corner. Discovery was but moments away. Certainly Rafferty didn't have the time to address Bryce's contempt for him.

He still dallied for several heartbeats, wondering how he could move a man who hated him so much he wouldn't look at him until, with an irritated slap of a fist against his thigh, he moved away. He reached the far corner, where he stopped.

Bryce's snort of derision cut through the night, suggesting that even though Rafferty had done his bidding, that only proved he'd been right about him.

Then it was too late to act; shapes were moving in the dark and there were too many for Rafferty to tackle alone. He scooted around the corner and then hurried away from the Lone Star saloon, losing himself in the shadows.

Behind him gunfire roared, followed by silence, followed by another burst. Then cries of discovery and triumph sounded.

Feeling wretched despite having acted in the only possible way, Rafferty decided to be cautious. He avoided the spot where he could see the stables and gave the town a wide berth.

He had seen everything he needed to. With him and Bryce having at least reduced the forces that were set against them, he now needed Tex's help.

In the dark it took him a while to find the route he'd taken to reach town, and the moon was at its highest point when he eventually saw the remembered grouping of boulders and then the wagon.

It stood quietly and he hoped Tex had got enough rest for him to be fit enough to help him, as he doubted George Milligan and the others would be alive come sunup.

At the wagon he leaned back against the side, gathering his breath. Then he tapped the wood.

'Tex,' he whispered, 'it's time to go.'

Silence was his answer, so he raised himself and looked inside. The wagon was empty.

It took only a moment's investigation to confirm

that Tex had gone, and the broken boards on the other side of the wagon showed who had taken him.

CHAPTER 15

'You can't even stand up,' Creswell Washington said when Tex was placed before him. 'Who brought you to Diamond Springs?'

Tex didn't reply immediately. Instead, he glanced around the stables. The massive Bud was holding him up and without his help he would slump to the ground.

Earlier, at the wagon, Bud had arrived quietly and then disarmed him before Tex had been able to mount a challenge. Then he'd tossed him over a shoulder, thankfully in a position that didn't put pressure on his wounded side, and brought him here.

Tex had been too weak to resist or to test Rafferty's theories about his captor. The matter-of-fact manner in which Bud had dealt with him confirmed that Rafferty was right that he followed orders without question.

As Bud was carrying out Creswell's orders, Tex reckoned Rafferty was probably wrong about him knowing more than he let on.

During Tex's quick appraisal of the situation in the stables, he noted that George Milligan had been tied to a post in the middle of the area. The prisoner was struggling to maintain a resolute expression as he awaited the inevitable interrogation.

Tex's capture appeared to extinguish his last hope as he looked at him with blank eyes.

Eight other men were dotted around the room, some others were outside, although Tex had noted one dead man, suggesting that Elias Sutherland had already launched a largely ineffective assault. But that had now ended as the badly beaten Elias was lying beside the door.

That was the only aspect of his appraisal that pleased him, and that pleasure was short-lived as the two other men who had left Bear Creek with Elias were also being kept prisoner.

This meant that the only hope lay in the two men as yet unaccounted for still being in a position to help. That hope receded when Sheriff Bryce's holed body was dragged inside after him.

'That's the man who helped me,' Tex said, waving a weak hand at Bryce.

'Why would a lawman help a man like you?' Creswell said.

Tex shrugged. 'Because we both want to stop you.'

'And one of you died in the attempt, while the other one will do so after he's witnessed my triumph.'

'That won't happen. You won't get your hands on the Lone Star.'

Creswell's snorted his breath through his nostrils, his brief display of temper confirming that he hadn't got to it yet.

'Obliged you reminded me,' Creswell said, regaining his usual controlled demeanour. He pointed at Bud. 'Throw Tex over there. Then get to work on George.'

Tex's shoulders rolled as Bud bent him over. Then Bud carried out his order in a literal fashion.

Creswell's men laughed as Tex's feet left the ground and then, for what felt like several seconds, he went flying through the air until he slammed into the wall. He crunched down on to his side and lay moaning.

Creswell's brief warning had given Tex enough time to ensure he fell on his unharmed side. Even so, he lay where he'd come to rest and didn't need to feign being hurt.

Then, in short order, two guards flanked him while Bud turned his attention on to George, who looked elsewhere, as if by not meeting his eye, he would save himself.

Slowly, Bud bunched a massive fist and, with mock gentleness, he brought the fist up to George's face. He tapped his chin, but the blow was still strong enough to crack his head back against the post.

'Stop!' George shouted, 'I don't know—'

He didn't get to complete his refusal to co-operate as Bud then slapped his right cheek with a resounding thud while again moving only slowly. A follow up slap to the left cheek jerked his head the other way.

Creswell came forward, making Bud back away.

'As you can see,' Creswell said, 'Bud can make this a long and painful night for you without breaking sweat. If I order him to put in some effort, he could break every bone in your body before—'

'You're wrong about me,' George said, desperation making his eyes wide and terrified. 'I don't know nothing about the diamond. I can never tell you anything, just like Elias and the others can't. None of us knows what Loudon Sutherland did with it.'

Creswell walked back and forth twice before he swung round to face George. He smiled.

'I know,' he whispered.

George had already opened his mouth to continue protesting, but when Creswell's comment registered, he closed it and considered him.

'Then why are you doing this to me?'

'To make you do one thing.' Creswell moved backward for two paces. He stopped where he could keep both Bud and George in view. 'Give Bud the order that only a man from Diamond Springs can.'

Tex couldn't help but look at Bud to see his reaction. He didn't notice one, but George's guilty expression was obvious and it convinced Tex that Rafferty had been right about his huge and silent assistant.

'What order?' George said without conviction.

Creswell chuckled. 'It's ironic, isn't it? Bud will do anything he's told and so, without difficulty, he's protected Loudon's secret for the last two years. And he'll continue to protect it for the rest of his life, but only if you can stop yourself from giving him a new order while he tears you apart.'

George gulped and cringed back against the post. He looked around for help, but as he faced only stern glares, he looked at Bud.

'Bud,' he said, with a pronounced gulp, 'Loudon gave you an order two years ago which, it seems, only I can countermand. I won't do that, so make it quick.'

Bud gave a slight inclination of the head and then moved in making George close his eyes while mouthing words to himself, presumably a prayer.

When Bud took another pace, Creswell gathered his intent and, with a muttered oath, he took long paces to stand between them. Bud brushed him aside with no discernible effort. Then he swung back a huge fist ready to club George with a swiping blow that would surely kill him.

A cry went up. 'No!'

To Tex's surprise, Bud stilled his hand and stood poised with his hand thrust back. Creswell righted himself and then looked up at Bud's face, his astonished expression showing he hadn't given the command.

Tex registered where the order had come from at the same moment as everyone else did. All eyes turned to the back of the stables and then looked upward.

There, on the hayloft twenty feet up, Rafferty Horn was standing. He had placed his legs wide apart and he sported a confident smile despite the overwhelming odds he faced below.

Rafferty's gaze sought out Tex and he winked before he hurried into hiding behind a short length of wall. A moment later Creswell got over his surprise and pointed up at the hayloft.

'Take him,' he shouted. 'I don't need that one alive.'

His men wasted no time in moving into positions facing the hayloft, but none of them would be able to get a clear sighting of Rafferty in his effective, albeit cornered, position.

Unless someone got in a lucky shot, one of Creswell's men would have to risk climbing a rickety ladder. Creswell wasted no time in picking out that man. He, with a resigned glance around at his colleagues, moved forward cautiously.

'And I don't need you alive either, Creswell,' Rafferty shouted from behind the wall.

The taunt encouraged two men to waste shots at

the hayloft before Creswell shouted at them to stop. Then he gestured at the man at the bottom of the ladder to start climbing.

When he put a foot on the bottom rung, Tex swung his legs beneath him and got to his knees. The motion wasn't noticed by his two guards, who were watching the hayloft.

As the situation was locked in a stalemate for now, Tex decided he could pick his moment to act. In the middle of the stables, George was craning his neck to look at the hayloft while Bud stood immobile.

As if he'd sensed that Tex was looking at them, Creswell also recognized the danger that Bud could present. He backed away from Bud to move outside the range of his long arms.

'Bud,' he said, pointing to the wall, 'stand over there and await further instructions.'

Bud didn't move, or even register that he'd been given an order. When long moments had passed, during which time Creswell glared at him with his face becoming redder, it was George's turn to smile.

'He's not listening to you, Creswell,' he said.

'Bud has always followed my orders,' Creswell snapped, his loud voice making the man on the ladder stop climbing to look at him.

'You're right, but the one thing you've never understood about Bud is that his friends always come first.'

'That's not the way he thinks. He does as he's told.'

'He does, and he's doing that now.' George laughed. 'Loudon ordered him to reveal the truth about the Lone Star only after one small thing had happened.'

'Which is?' Creswell asked with a pronounced gulp.

George whispered his answer, his words being uttered too low for Tex to hear as, at that moment, gunfire tore out.

Rafferty must have been able to see enough of the scene below to know that the situation had become less certain for Creswell, as he'd come out from behind his covering wall on his knees. He blasted an accurate shot down at the man on the ladder that caught his shoulder and sent him tumbling to the ground.

That encouraged the rest of Creswell's men to lay down a sustained burst of gunfire at the hayloft and this time Creswell didn't order them to stop. Instead, he backed away again with his gaze darting between George and Bud.

His expression was an inscrutable one which, after another two paces, Tex understood.

George's whispered answer had worried him, perhaps even scared him, and the unusual emotion was making him less assured than usual. Tex decided to add to his problems.

With a hand clutched to his chest, he clambered up to a crouched position and then slowly raised himself. He was bent double when his motion caught the attention of the guard to his right.

Tex abandoned caution and raised himself as quickly as he could. He was still slow and he doubted he could overwhelm even one guard. So he carried out the only action he had the strength to do: he barged into the right-hand guard with a leading shoulder. Unfortunately, the blow was even weaker than he'd feared it would be and he merely leaned against his target.

The guard stood his ground with ease. Worse, the second guard swung round and from behind slapped two firm hands on Tex's shoulders, which buckled his legs.

Tex thrust out a hand to the wall to stop himself falling, but the effort failed when, in his weak state, his flailing hand only reached as far as the guard's chest.

As he fell, he grabbed a handful of the man's jacket. Then he plummeted like a dead weight. His quick descent dragged the guard down with him and the man landed sprawled over Tex's back, flattening him to the ground.

As Tex lay on the ground feeling too weak even to attempt to throw the guard off him, Creswell shouted an order that he couldn't hear. Then a prolonged burst of gunfire ripped out across the stables.

The guard shifted position as he moved to get off him and his movements caused his hip to press into

Tex's unwounded side. For the first time since he'd been captured, Tex couldn't help but smile.

Acting blindly, he twisted his left wrist and felt for the man's holster, touching leather at the first attempt. Then, when the guard pushed himself up from Tex's back, he left without his gun.

As Tex reckoned this would be his only chance he gritted his teeth and rolled over, twisting his hips to make sure he landed on the same spot. The action sent a jolt of pain tearing through his chest, but he ended up lying on his back with the gun aimed upwards.

A moment later two quick shots tore out. The first slug took his opponent in the stomach, making him crumple, while the second shot took the other guard high in the chest.

Before that man had hit the ground, Tex pushed himself back to the wall to rest while he sought out his next target.

So much gunfire was blasting out that Creswell wasn't looking his way. Instead, he was dividing his attention between the assault on the hayloft and Bud, who had now moved on to stand beside George.

Tex reckoned Creswell could wait; he jerked his gun to the side and peppered a deadly rain of lead at the backs of Creswell's men until he was forced to gather bullets from the first guard he had shot and was able to reload.

As man after man went down, Creswell reacted at

last to the new threat and swung round to face him. Tex smiled, simulating a confidence he was yet to feel.

'Time to pay, Creswell,' he said as he punched in the first slug.

'For you it is,' Creswell said. He pointed a firm finger at him. 'Take him!'

Tex kept calm and continued to punch in bullets. Thankfully, Creswell's men were still seeking to flush Rafferty out and they didn't react immediately.

Creswell shouted out the order again as behind him George whispered to Bud. Tex hoped that Bud would then attack Creswell, but instead, he put two hands to the post that was securing George. He tugged.

The post shook making George look aloft and wince, but despite his concern, Bud tugged the post again, making the wood screech in protest. Tex couldn't see what had worried George, so he slipped in the final slug.

Then he looked at Creswell's men. Despite Creswell's order, they weren't paying him any attention. Most of them were cringing down and several were pointing directly upwards.

Tex assumed that Rafferty had now acted decisively, but he wasn't visible, so Tex strained his neck to look higher. He winced, seeing now what had worried everyone.

The post that secured George went up to the roof

and, as it stood in the centre of the stables, it was a supporting part of the structure.

Dust rained down, then splinters of wood, then whole planks. At last, with a huge crack, the post split down its length. The two pieces toppled to the side and took George with them.

The whole building shook, making Tex slide to the side as the wall at his back shifted position. The standing men wavered back and forth as they struggled to decide which direction would give them the best chance of surviving, but they were already too late; the building was collapsing.

'Get out!' Creswell shouted, his order being unnecessary as everyone had abandoned the gunfight to concentrate on self-preservation.

As the roof was already coming down in a series of shuddering crashes, Tex didn't reckon he could get out in time so he chose to complete his mission instead. He levelled his gun on Creswell and enjoyed his last few moments by squeezing the trigger slowly.

Creswell had turned to the door, so he would hit him in the back. That didn't matter to Tex and it mattered even less when, before he could fire, a gunshot blasted. Creswell grunted in pain then staggered sideways before he dropped to his knees.

He righted himself and fought to twist his head so he could look at Tex. Anger contorted his face and blood dribbled from his chest.

The sight made Tex smile. A moment later Tex

planted another two quick bullets in Cresswell's side before he looked to the hayloft.

Rafferty was standing up, keeping his balance by placing a hand on the wall that he'd been hiding behind. He still had his smoking gun aimed at Creswell. When his target didn't move, he looked at Tex. Each man nodded to the other.

'Save Tex,' Rafferty shouted. Then the roof fell against the hayloft and he disappeared from view.

Despite his earlier treachery, Tex wished him well. Then he did the only thing he could do: he curled up into a ball and lay on his side.

Darkness loomed above him and he looked up expecting to see the roof falling in on him. It was, but standing over him was the large form of Bud. He'd spread his arms, making himself into a human shield to protect Tex from the falling debris.

'Save yourself,' Tex said, meeting his gaze.

Bud gave a slight shake of the head. Then the roof slammed down on his back.

CHAPTER 16

'You fine, Rafferty?' Elias Sutherland asked, the question being accompanied by an insistent slapping of Rafferty's face that suggested he'd been unconscious for a while.

'I will be if you stop hitting me,' Rafferty said.

He opened his eyes to find that Elias was kneeling beside him. He was bloodied and one swollen eye was closed, but he was smiling.

More surprisingly, sufficient time had passed for an arc of light to lighten the eastern horizon. Rafferty raised himself on to an elbow, finding to his delight that he could move easily and without pain.

He saw that he'd been dragged away from the collapsed stables and then deposited on the patch of ground where earlier he had planned his desperate assault. Several bodies were lying near by and he looked at each one until he saw Creswell's.

'Flattened,' Elias said, 'after he'd been shot several

times. I guess his ignominious end might be a comfort to my brother.'

'And to the rest.'

Rafferty looked around and, guessing his concern, Elias pointed to the north.

'The men who worked for Creswell were hired guns and the survivors were too dazed to have any fight left in them, especially as the man who was paying them had died. They fled.'

'And who didn't get out?'

'I was too weak to be much use, but I reckon we got to them all, either alive or dead.' Elias pointed behind him. 'We had effective help with the rescue.'

Rafferty shuffled round and saw that Bud was sitting on the ground a few yards behind him. His back was bowed and he was ruefully rubbing a shoulder as he stared at the stables with his usual expressionless air.

Rafferty had never seen Bud show any sign of suffering before, so he reckoned he must be in pain, but he was alive and that was more than anyone could have expected when the building had come down.

Just as heartening was the sight of George and Tex sitting beside Bud, and the casual way Elias glanced at Tex suggested that, while he'd been unconscious, they had come to an understanding.

Tex had adopted the same relaxed posture as Rafferty and he acknowledged him with a salute before he turned his gaze again to the stables, a hand clutched to his ribs.

'It's good that Bear Creek will be free of Creswell's clutches,' Tex said after a while.

'And it's good for the men he killed,' Rafferty said, 'that he didn't find the Lone Star.'

'Sure,' Tex said with a sigh, 'not that we did either.'

Rafferty winced. 'Do you mean that Bud doesn't know what happened to it, after all?'

Tex looked at Bud and waited for him to reply, but when he stayed quiet, he stood and worked his way around him. He sat down beside Rafferty and then snorted a rueful laugh before he leaned towards him with a conspiratorial smile on his lips.

'He does know. Loudon Sutherland ordered him to hide it somewhere where nobody would ever find it.'

Tex glanced at Elias, who completed the story.

'And,' he said, 'to speak of what he'd done only after Creswell was dead. That was why I hired Tex, and in the end he completed his mission.'

Neither man said anything more. Rafferty nodded, accepting that even though he could never support Loudon's sacrifice, Loudon had given it an appropriate twist that would have annoyed Creswell had he learned the truth. He looked past Tex at Bud and raised an eyebrow.

'You can speak now, Bud,' he said. 'Where did you hide the Lone Star?'

Bud turned from his contemplation of the stables to face him. He took a while to reply, as was appropriate for an order that had taken two years to complete.

'I ate it,' he said simply.

Rafferty waited to see if there was more of an explanation to come, but Bud turned away. So Rafferty joined him and the other men in looking down at the stables.

Then his gaze moved away from the stables to rest on another abandoned and yet once popular building behind the Lone Star saloon. He began wondering, as the others would already be doing, whether he wanted to find the Lone Star diamond badly enough to begin an altogether different kind of search.

As the dawn approached and the last bright star above winked out of existence, he laughed.

Before long, the others joined him. Bud laughed the hardest.